HOW THE WITCH STOLE CHRISTMAS

DAKOTA CASSIDY

same name or names. Any similarities to real persons, situations, or incidents is purely coincidental.

ISBN: 9781720136729

Imprint: Independently published

ACKNOWLEDGMENTS

Dear Fabulous, Amazing, Awesome readers,

Please note, the Witchless in Seattle series is truly best read in order, to understand the full backstory and history of each character as they develop with every connecting book.

Especially in the case of the mystery surrounding Winterbottom (I know it drives some of you crazy. Sorrysorrysorry!). His story is ever evolving and will contain some mini-cliffhangers from book to book. But I promise not to make you wait too long until I answer each set of questions I dredge up.

I also promise the central mystery featured in each addition to the series will always be wrapped up with a big bow by book's end!

That said, I hope you'll join me for *Ain't Love A Witch?*, Book 6 in the series, and *Witch, Please!*, Book 7, coming in 2017!

No matter how you arrived here, thanks so much for joining Stevie and company on their journey to solve afterlife mysteries, and her search to regain her witchy powers.

From myself, Stevie, Belfry, Winterbottom, Whiskey and all the Ebenezer Falls gang (living and dead), here's to a joyous holiday season, filled with all the things you love, and a healthy, prosperous New Year!

Happy holidays to all!
Dakota XXOO

HOW THE WITCH STOLE CHRISTMAS

BY DAKOTA CASSIDY

CHAPTER 1

"Oh, Mr. Butterbaum, you didn't...?" I asked, knowing the answer before he nodded his snowy-white head to confirm.

He blustered, leaning back in his chair and brushing a hand over his houndstooth jacket with the cheerfully blinking Santa pin on his lapel.

"I didn't mean to... Honest. She was so dang mad at me, too. She before I could tell her I was sorry. I need to apologize, Stevie...er, I mean, Madam Zoltar, or whatever we're callin' ya these days. I need my girl to know I'm sorry. Maybe that'll give her some peace and she'll stop showin' up at the end of my bed every night, holdin' that durn," he threw up his fingers in quotes, "'special sucky hose thing' attachment. Scares the livin' boxers right off'a me every time, I tell you."

I readjusted my signature Madam Zoltar turban and gripped his hand, giving him a pensive glance. I couldn't help but wonder what provoked him to buy a vacuum as a gift.

"But a *vacuum*? You bought your one and only true love a *vacuum* for Christmas? Her last Christmas here on earth?"

I sighed and fought a judgmental frown. *Men.* Though, in Mr. B's defense, maybe his wife had wanted one.

"It *was* the Shark," he weakly defended with a sheepish glance peppered with guilt, making the wrinkles beside each of his eyes deepen. "I thought I was doing good by her. Matilda even said she wanted one. Swear she did while she was watchin' an infomercial for it. Said she'd like to have one." He shook his head in remorse. "Knew I shoulda gone with the dang Pajama Jeans. Now she's hauntin' me and I don't know what to do. Don't only spirits who haven't crossed over do that? You gotta help her, Stevie—and me, too. Ain't slept a whole night through in forever."

"May I ask question?"

"Mmmm," I muttered back to one of my beloved afterlife pals.

"Arkady Bagrov does not understand why a sucky Shark hose thing is not a good thing," my favorite dead Russian spy said, clearly oblivious to the matters of women. "Where I come from, giving the sucky thing is high praise. This Matilda should be grateful her husband give her something so useful to make his home beautiful, no?"

I fought a laugh, using the back of my hand to cover

my mouth while not revealing to Mr. Butterbaum I was hearing a ghost praise his choice of the ultimate Christmas gift.

Now Win's good-natured laughter barked in my ear. "Ahhh, old chap. I'd say *nyet*. But this of course explains why you could never have a wife. Women want something with true meaning. Something you've invested a moment of research on, you old goat. Not a vacuum with a special sucky thing."

Arkady's rumble of good cheer followed Win's remark. "Hah! You!" he playfully accused. "You should know about the sucky thing. This silly talk of meaningful gifts is what you call the sucking *up* thing!"

And then Win laughed in return, something that happened a great deal since he and Arkady had met up again in the afterlife a few months ago during the hottest week we'd ever had on record here in Ebenezer Falls, Washington. Once mortal enemies, now buddies, they often slapped each other on the back like old friends these days.

Which was nice, considering Arkady had joined our little family in his direct, or what some would call, pushy manner. He just showed up one day while I was in the height of a confrontation with who we now know was Win's twin brother, Balthazar (more on him and his dastardly disappearance later), inserted himself into our lives, and never left.

Since then, I'd come to love hearing Arkady's rich voice, his swoon-worthy accent, and even his completely unfiltered sexist thoughts. He genuinely

3

doesn't mean to be so insensitive. On the contrary, he's quite complimentary to me in my ongoing spy training —holds me in the highest regard for being nothing more than, according to him, a mere mortal with more grit and determination than ten Russian spies in a Siberian prison.

But unintentional sexist comments aside, he's kind and giving, and above all, loyal to us to the core, and that helps when it comes time to speak to the spirits. He, like Win, aids me in contacting the dead at my little shop here in the center of Ebenezer Falls. He proves quite helpful when dealing with the crustier-than-usual specters.

With his stern reminders he once took on a cartel in Mexico with nothing more than a Chapstick and a can of pickled herring, and his cheerfully forceful way of pushing the more tight-lipped ghosts to ante up information, he's a good addition to our small crew of ghostly facilitators.

Oh, and he seems to make Win really happy. Win, my dead British secret agent, stuck on what we jokingly call Plane Limbo (a plane where, after death, the undecided go), deserved a friend to share his afterlife.

This particular plane can become quite lonely as spirits come and go with rapid frequency and they decide whether to cross over, making it tough for those who aren't ready to cross to forge friendships.

For the moment, Arkady was sticking around, and he and Win spent lots of time together rehashing old spy missions, and in general behaving like they were back in high school, reliving their glory days.

Whiskey, our rescue St. Bernard, stirred at my feet, tucking his nose against my calf, reminding me Mr. Butterbaum was still waiting to speak to Matilda, his recently passed wife of over fifty years.

"Mr. Butterbaum?"

He patted my hand, his gnarled fingers curling over mine, his face a mass of worried wrinkles. "Call me Vern, MZ."

I smiled in sympathy. "All right. Vern it is. So let me get this right. You want to apologize to your wife for buying her a vacuum for Christmas."

He dipped his head at me. "Yep. That'll exorcise her, right? Or whatever ya call it. Make her go into the light? I want her to rest in peace is all."

Fighting a chuckle, I wondered if the vacuum was really the problem here. "Yes, my goal is to help her cross over into the light, but do you really think she was that angry over a vacuum cleaner? Angry enough to haunt you? You were married for fifty years. Surely she knows you well enough to know you meant well by giving her a vacuum with a special hose attachment."

"Then why does she keep showin' up every night at the end of our bed, wavin' that hose attachment thing around like a checkered flag at the Indy 500?"

"That is the question." I patted his arm and squeezed it tight, holding up Matilda's treasured locket between the fingers of my other hand. Sometimes, making contact with the dearly departed was easier if I had a personal object they'd worn or some item they truly loved. "Are you ready, Vern?"

He puffed his chest out as though preparing to put on a brave front and gave me a hesitant smile. "I think so."

Settling back in my Madam Zoltar chair, I said, "Dim the lights, please," voice-activating our lighting system. Instantly, the lights settled into an amber glow, making Vern's fresh-from-Florida-golfing-trip tan appear deeper. "Matilda? Are you here with us, dear? I have someone who'd like to talk to you."

The light hum of energy I felt when a presence announced itself had been growing stronger as of late. The shiver along my spine indicating an aura in the room occurred just like the days of old, before I had my witch powers slapped out of me by a vengeful warlock.

Each time I performed a séance during the summer months, when our tourist season here in Ebenezer Falls was at its highest, I'd experienced some of my old signals, and I welcomed them—relished them—but mostly, I tried not to dwell on them.

It was almost as if, if I ignored the possible return of my powers, I couldn't end up disappointed if they didn't fully return. In my old life as a witch, before I'd been shunned, I'd lived in a town where the paranormal lived out in the open. I'd also communicated with the dead, it was my specialty. I heard them speak to me as though they were right in the room, and then one day I didn't.

The loss of that communication had been devastating—but the miracle of hearing Win, and more recently Arkady, were promising signs all hope wasn't lost. But I wasn't going to count my chickens just yet. I couldn't for fear of crushing defeat.

"Matilda?" I called again as the hum became deeper, more resonant, and the Christmas lights we'd strung around the room began to flicker. I smiled at Vern, whose eyes had grown wider than dimes. "I think she's here, Vern."

I was excited by this prospect. Vern? Well, Vern, obviously not so much. He sat hunkered down in his chair, his shoulders bunched together.

Win cleared his throat. "I have contact, Dove. Matilda's here with me."

"She's here, Vern. Go ahead and say whatever you'd like to say."

Vern blustered, his bushy white eyebrows scrunching together when he scanned the room as though his wife might pop out of the ether, hose attachment in hand.

"Matilda, honey? I'm sorry. I don't know why you're showin' up every night, but I need my sleep, gal, for our grandkids, and you're scarin' the ever-livin' poop right outta me, all hovering and looming with that dang hose. I don't know what you want me to do. How many more times do you want me to apologize?"

Patting his hand, I silently reassured him he'd done well.

"Matilda says to tell Vern she hovers and looms because something's stuck in the hose, and he'd know that if he vacuumed himself instead of paying that lushly ripe peach of a Happy Housekeeper, Jeanette Hartman, to do it. Then she called him a moron," Win offered with a deep chuckle. "Affectionately, of course."

Every once in a while, when a spirit from the afterlife wasn't really hurting anyone, when the situation wasn't dire, I told fibs as I relayed messages. Not big ones, mind you, but some dipped in a little more sugar than vinegar.

So, I nodded my head to signal to Win I understood. "Vern? Matilda says there's something stuck in the hose. She's been trying to tell you, and that's why she keeps showing up each night."

Now, Vern looked affronted, almost annoyed, his lips pursing as he squinted his eyes. "Well, what the heck, gal? What's stuck in the hose that's so important you gotta show up every night, spookin' the life outta me?"

"Now, Matilda, don't say such things." Win clucked his fancy British admonishment. "Vern simply wants you to find peace. Forget about the Happy Housekeeper and play nice with us now, darling. Tell us what troubles you so."

I followed Win's lead and asked, "Matilda? What's stuck in the vacuum hose? Vern wants to know. Won't you please share?"

"Yessiree, he does," Vern assured the room, his eyes squinting. "'Fore he has a heart attack."

"Ahhh," Win whispered, his husky voice echoing in

my ear. "I see. How lovely, Matilda. Won't that be a brilliant gift? Something to always remember you by."

"What's that, Matilda?" I encouraged Win to pass on what Matilda told him, cocking my ear to the room.

"Matilda says it's her wedding ring. She wants to be sure their granddaughter has it before her wedding to her beau in early spring. She meant to tell Vern if anything happened to her, to give it to her, but she passed in her sleep before she was able."

"Oh, Matilda, what a lovely thing to do," I murmured, my throat tightening.

"She also says to please apologize to Vern for the misunderstanding. She wasn't angry about the gift at all. She quite adored the vacuum. In fact, it worked so well, she accidentally vacuumed up the ring by mistake. She'd forgotten to put it back on after applying some hand lotion and knocked it from their dresser. By appearing to him each night, she was only trying to ensure their granddaughter had the ring as promised."

Nodding, I smiled at Vern and explained the circumstances of the ring. "Matilda also says she loved the gift, but most of all she loves you, and can't wait to see you again."

Vern's shoulders shook a little beneath his suit jacket then, his eyes becoming watery discs of blue. "She's okay, my girl? She's happy?" he asked, his voice tremulous.

"She is, Vern. So very happy," I replied, biting the inside of my cheek to keep a small sob from escaping.

Pulling a neat square of a handkerchief with reindeer on it from his inside shirt pocket, Vern mopped at his eyes. "I love you, gal. Love you bigger than the moon and stars. You go on now. I'll meet ya there," he said, his gruff voice cracking.

The room stilled suddenly, as though all the air evaporated from the space. The lights flickered, casting long shadows on the walls of the room we called, in tribute to Madam Zoltar, my predecessor, Séance Command Central.

And then, as though expelling a breath, a soft warmth whispered throughout, floating across the table where we sat, making the lights warmer, the candles flames jump higher and the scent of magnolias drift to my nose.

I knew before Win said as much, but hearing his confirmation made me smile anyway. "She's gone over, Dove. As easy as any crossing we've had."

Sighing in happiness as the room returned to normal, I gripped Vern's hand and squeezed. "She's gone, Vern. Safely on the other side."

He let his head hang low, his chin dropping to his chest. "Sure do miss her."

A tear escaped my eye, the way it always did when a spirit found eternal peace, as I nodded my understanding. "She loved you very much, Vern."

Fifty years was a long time to remain with one person, but their bond reminded me true love existed, across all kinds of boundaries—even death.

Vern's head snapped up as he straightened his jacket and clapped my hand in a final thump, his crooked fingers wrapping around mine before letting go. "When ya find yourself a good fellow, you hang on tight, ya hear, Stevie? There ain't nothin' like it. Have a merry Christmas, Toots."

Rising from his chair, he put on his hat, dropped some bills on the table we'd donate to our various causes, and was gone, the chilly wind from Puget Sound blowing into the door as he pulled it open and left.

I folded my hands in front of me on the table and let my forehead rest against them, absorbing the last remainders of Matilda's soul, allowing her passing a moment of respectful silence.

"Every day, I'm thinking I like you more, Stevie," Arkady whispered, his tone as gruff as Vern's had been.

"You know what I'm thinking, comrade?" I asked, pushing the chair away from the table.

"What is this you are thinking, my little slice of lemon meringue pie?"

I snickered. Arkady had a million nicknames for me, most of them having to do with food, which Win assured me was our Russian spy friend's downfall. At one point on a mission in the Alps, Win declared Arkady had grown too out of shape to chase him properly.

"I'm thinking the hour is late and we need to get home to Bel and see how the setup for the neighborhood open house and Christmas Lights Display Contest is going. I haven't heard from him in over three hours, but I promised I wouldn't micromanage this whole thing. Yet, I worry I haven't timed the lights to blink in tune with 'All I Want for Christmas' just right. It needs tweaking. Not to mention, 'Christmas Time Is Here' has to play at the exact moment the judges enter the house. I want them to see the amazing spread of food I've planned, and be filled with the peace and joy of the season."

"Heaven forbid they aren't at peace as they dine on authentic French pastries that stuffy sod, Chef Foo-Foo Wahoo's concocted. Wasn't it he who said, 'I am ze best chef in ze world! Ask anyone and he will tell you, Chef Foo-Foo Wahoo makes pastries lighter zan ze air itself!'"

I snorted my endless amusement with the fact that Win wasn't a fan of our local caterer, Petula's, new pastry chef and boyfriend. "His name is Chef Pascal Le June, Spy Guy, and it's important the judges enjoy their moment with us—feast on the goodies we've had prepared as they rest in the lull of the amazing Christmas storm I've whipped up. We want to stand out, don't we?"

"Hah! If the judges' souls aren't in complete harmony with the universe because of Chef Foo-Foo's 'lighter than air itself' pastries, surely Norman Reedus himself will scream in, covered in Georgia sweat and filth, crossbow at his shoulder, dead squirrel on a stick to tell us the apocalypse has arrived."

My giggle filled the store at Win's disgust for Chef Le June. I thought he'd be pleased as a Brit in the Queen's service to see I'd actually hired someone with so much experience and world-renowned praise. My Spy Guy was a bit of a snob when it came to food and his luxuries. So his distaste for Chef Le June left me confounded.

One of my eyebrows rose in mock disdain. "This from a man who hired Cirque du Soleil acrobats and mimes to perform at our housewarming party? Quit poo-pooing my chef, pal, and remind yourself where I learned to hire only the best. *From* the best. That would be *you*. I learned from you. Now we need to make haste, boys. We have less than an hour before the judges arrive."

Setting my turban on the table, I began blowing out candles and looking for my purse, spurred on by the fact I hadn't heard from Bel, and all the little details I'd planned so carefully had to be checked and double-checked.

Vern's séance had been the last of the season for us. Madam Zoltar 2.0 was officially going on a two-week holiday break because she had big Christmas plans.

Have I mentioned it's almost Christmas here in Eb Falls? Have I also mentioned it's, without a doubt, my absolute favorite holiday of all time?

Well, it is, and this year, much like Clark Griswold from *Christmas Vacation*, with not just Win, Whiskey and Arkady, but both my parents in the picture, I was determined to make it the best Christmas ever, with all the trimmings.

I know, I know. I'm an ex-witch. You're probably wondering why Halloween isn't my favorite holiday.

Swear, I'm not holding a grudge or anything like that. I mean, over the loss of my witch powers and being booted from my coven. I can only say, even before I was shunned, the thrill of ghosts and goblins and spooky cemeteries dries up a little when you deal with them on a daily basis.

Either way, today was the beginning of my hiatus from the store until after the New Year.

And I was starting with the Eb Falls Christmas Lights Display Contest. I was going to win that bad boy and nab that trophy if it took feeding stray souls to puppies.

I kid. Mostly, anyway. I really do want to win. I don't know why the contest had become my eye of the tiger. I'm not normally overly competitive, but no one is better at creating magic with a set of Christmas lights than I am. Ask anyone in my old hometown of Paris, Texas, just how good I am at hanging lights and turning old barns into winter wonderlands.

I'd been planning, and Pinteresting, and making flow charts, and drawing diagrams for months since I'd heard about this contest at the Eb Falls potluck dinner I'd gone to with Forrest at the church back in September. I'd paid close attention to the rules designed to keep things fair amongst neighbors.

Each participating homeowner had a budget we had to adhere to (I think that rule was made up especially for me. My fellow Eb Fall-ers worried out loud I'd have more to spend on decorations—due to my much-speculated millionaire status—and I'd go overboard. Hah! I can decorate on a budget like nobody's business). We couldn't bring in any professional designers, we had to do the work ourselves, and we weren't allowed any live animal nativities.

According to Forrest—my occasional date, and grandson to my favorite senior Ebenezer Falls resident, Chester Sherwood—one year, in desperation, Alma Sandford had stolen Lars McKinnon's old cow Bessie-Lou, after her own cow had the audacity to up and die two days before the contest.

Anyway, I'd orchestrated music timed with lights, snowmen, reindeer, bells, Santa on my rooftop, and even fireworks. *That* was my pista resistance (yes, I know it's pièce de résistance. But this sounds funnier, yes? At least Bel and I think so), my ace in the hole. The fireworks display with Santa throwing glitter from his bag of booty. I tingled all over just thinking about it.

Each contestant participating also hosted an open house for the judges, complete with all sorts of yummy holiday goodies they could snack on to keep their energy levels high as they handled the exhausting chore of their judging duties. Hence Chef Le June.

I think I rolled my eyes when Mrs. Vanderhelm, the head of the Eb Falls Christmas parade and planning board, fed us that line, but I didn't care. I'd hired someone to handle the tempting tasties so I could focus on my real mission, making this holiday the best one ever.

Or maybe it was the best first *real* Christmas with

all the trimmings ever, like family and friends and decorations and platter after platter of delicious food.

Most Christmases, it was just Bel, me, The Hallmark Channel, and the occasional invite to a friend's house. I'd never had the opportunity to spend it with my father because he hadn't come into the picture until just this year. And my mother?

Well, let's just say, before Dita began to make this miraculous change in her life this past spring, she hadn't been around much in my adult life, and when I was a child, she'd never made much ado about Christmas.

So, if I'm honest, this year was about making up for all the Christmases past. The ones where I watched holiday shows about families who decorated trees together, went on sleigh rides, drank hot coco, and gathered 'round a big table full of smiling faces on Christmas Day...but had none of those things.

This year, I had a family, and I wanted them all, living and dead, to know how much I loved them. How proud I was of their accomplishments. How much I treasured the chance to spend the holiday with them.

"You know," Win remarked casually as I hopped into my new replacement Fiat (see: total disaster last spring, when my first Fiat ended up in the drink). "Speaking of my old chap Belfry. I haven't heard from him since we arrived at the store either. Quite unusual, don't you think, Dove?"

"Bah!" Arkady barked as we sped away. "I bet my old heat-seeking missile days he is taking nap. I know my little comrade, and how much he likes to make with the Z's."

I chuckled as we headed out of town, admiring each small store's light display as we drove toward what I fondly called Mayhem Manor, our amazing, freshly renovated house set high on a cliff facing Puget Sound.

I loved our house, with its sprawling front porch, wide steps, all sorts of peaks and turrets, room after room of soft, muted colors and vintage furniture and, most of all, the incredible view. Decorating the house had been a dream come true for this Christmas lover, and I'd been working on it for over a month.

Everything should be in place by now. Every light display, every Santa and snowman, should all twinkle. The group of carolers I'd hired should be humming Nat King Cole along the front porch steps. And one of Petula's staff should have delivered Chef Le June's pastries, and the scent of hazelnut and chicory coffee, along with rich white hot chocolate with plump marshmallows and peppermint sticks, should be filling the air in our kitchen.

As we came around the bend of the road along my house, I waited to catch my breath and be astounded by the magnificent beauty of the Christmas I'd created in my imagination. Belfry had promised he'd have the lights on when I came home so I could preview all our hard work before the judges arrived and tweak any last-minute problems, should they arise.

"My daffodil of love?"

"Yeah, Arkady?"

"Why are you Americans all so strange?"

I frowned as an oncoming car's headlights temporarily blinded me. "What do you mean?"

"Look on the roof, my pumpkin seed. Arkady Bagrov wants to know, is this some new American Christmas tradition?"

As I pulled up to our long driveway, looking upward to see what Arkady meant, I too, wondered the same thing.

Because it definitely wasn't an American Christmas tradition I saw.

But the real question was, why—or better still, *how*—had a bright white light-up metal Easter bunny, with a big blue bow around his neck, ended up sitting on the roof of our house, spitting Easter eggs from his butt?

CHAPTER 2

J fell out of the car with a gasp, holding on to the door in a white-knuckled grip. I almost couldn't speak, but somehow I managed to croak, *"What the fudge?"*

"Bollocks!" Win yelped with surprise. "Are those *pink flamingos?*" He paused a moment, as though he, like me, couldn't believe his eyes, and then he inhaled a sharp breath. "They bloody well are! Eleven of them, if I'm counting right."

Win had absolutely counted right. There were exactly eleven pink, plastic flamingos on my lawn, all displayed in a crooked circle, the wind lashing at them so they clacked together in a plastic song of unison.

My eyes widened, almost glazing over as I took in the scene before me. *"What...?"*

"Now, now, my precious pearl of the sea," Arkady soothed, his voice like a gentle stroke to my back. "This is not so bad. Look at those beads the scantily clad

19

women are throwing from the balcony upstairs. Like during Mardi Gras, *da*? Aren't they colorful? I promise you, I have been to your New Orleans, and those beads are just as shiny."

Arkady was right. The beads the women were throwing from our upstairs balcony were very shiny— especially when they caught the glint of the hazy red-light district bulb glowing and revolving above their heads. Nine heads in total, if one were to calculate.

But hold up. *There were women throwing Mardi Gras beads from my guest-bedroom balcony.*

My breath shuddered in and out, the cold air pushing puffy clouds of condensation from my lips while I watched each woman twirl the beads around her fingers in saucy fashion, posing seductively and blowing kisses to an invisible audience.

Yet, still I couldn't summon words.

Win's warm presence surrounded me, attempting to invisibly hold me up. "Dove, gather yourself now. We must find Belfry and investigate what's gone so awry."

"*Awry?*" I fumed as air finally pushed its way back into my lungs. "Do you see this, Win? Something hasn't gone awry; it's gone bananapants! Off the rails! Look at this, Win! Where are all my decorations? This is a disaster!"

"In all fairness, I, like my old adversary Arkady, rather don't mind the women in corsets throwing beads. But I will admit, the witch with a wildly sparking wand planted firmly in her bum might come off as a bit garish and tasteless to some. Especially to that judge Mrs. Vanderhelm, whom I think we all know can certainly identify with the witch and her bum."

That would be funny if, one, it weren't true, and two, it weren't happening on my front lawn. I doubled over, gripping my stomach as each new horror of this redecorating nightmare prank presented itself. I almost couldn't take it all in. All the lights, the sound, the color.

Who had stolen all my Christmas decorations and, in their place, hung from every possible corner of our house everything *but* Christmas decorations?

Who?

Where had my decorations gone?

Where was the Santa, sliding down a hill on a sled, that I'd handcrafted myself from wire and lights after seeing a picture and directions on Pinterest? It had taken me a weekly class in welding in Seattle and nearly two days to position that darn thing on the roof so the judges would see it from the road.

Who'd replaced that with an Easter bunny pooping Easter eggs?

Where was the snowman family, playfully lobbing snowballs at each other in an arc of colored snowballs? Who had taken my daggone mechanical, life-size, Victorian-era Santa from the front porch and put a cackling, almost demonic-looking, equally life-size Uncle Sam with an out-of-control red sparkler in its place?

Why, instead of a softly glowing sign reading Merry

Christmas To All on the second-floor balcony over-hang, was there now a cheap, half-lit sign reading Eat At Bo-Bo's?

Where were the standing lanterns with festive greenery and shimmering gold and red ribbons lining the pathway to my front steps? Who had swapped them out for a single skinny scarecrow with a moth-eaten burlap shirt and a pile of rotted pumpkins?

It was then I made the mistake of looking to my left, where, in my hydrangea garden, should have resided the nativity.

The nativity I'd thrown all my love into? Trashed. The eyeball-rolling joy I'd derived from making those iconic figures out of papier mâché after watching videos on YouTube? History.

No!

Who, in good conscience, would steal my realistic baby Jesus and replace him instead with a zombie garden gnome, its gnashing teeth dripping blood? And the Virgin Mary with the light-up shawl? Someone had actually had the nerve to abscond with her and replace her with a cardboard cutout of Frankenstein posi-tioned just right, so he loomed over the baby Jesus imposter. And where in all of Sweet Pete was Joseph?

Was this some kind of joke Belfry was playing? Was he taking his revenge on me for being so picayune and difficult about this contest since I'd begun planning to coup a win from my entire neighborhood?

No. Never. Bel knew how much I wanted to win. Sure, he'd called me silly, he'd mocked me all while I'd learned to use a blowtorch and played in endless amounts of water and glue to get the right consistency for my papier mâché.

But he'd helped me every step of the way, too, indulged my every whim—even when I'd considered taking on the enormous task of personally acting out "The Twelve Days of Christmas" with partridges and everything.

No, someone had sabotaged me, and that someone was going to pay!

As I began to consider suspects, I heard a familiar tune—one I was sure I'd heard in some club back in the day. My whirling dervish of a mind stopped dead in its tracks and I groaned.

Why of all the why's in the wide-wide world were my twelve handpicked carolers tossing a multicolored beach ball around, dressed in corsets, bikinis, fishnet stockings, stilettos and Speedos, singing not "The Christmas Song," but "Pour Some Sugar On Me"—*with* handheld bells?

Just as I began to catch my breath, I saw something else that made me gasp and widen my eyes until they near fell out of my head.

"Is that...?" I began, but couldn't finish the sentence as I pointed to the front porch, where red and purple lights flashed out an angry, erratic beat.

"A stripper pole? I believe that's an affirmative, Dove," Win replied after a long silence, his voice much too calm for me.

Yes, indeed. It certainly was a stripper pole,

right in the middle of our front porch, complete with an admirably athletic woman in a red, sparkly thong bikini and the highest heels I've ever seen. She slid along the pole with such elongated grace, you'd think it didn't take the entirety of her estimated six hundred and thirty-nine muscles to do so.

Slamming the door of the car, I lifted the hem of my Madam Zoltar caftan and stomp-picked my way through a display of maudlin headstones (ten of them, if anyone was keeping track) with each of the Christmas Lights Display Contest judges' names on them.

"Belfry!" I bellowed into the darkening night. "What the heck's going on?"

Like he always did whenever they were separated, Whiskey bounded out ahead of me and up the steps to find his buddy Belfry, only to become caught up in a fake spider web attached on either side of each of the porch's pillars. He growled and struggled, twisting his large body as Win called out to him.

"Settle down, boy! Wait there for Stevie to untangle you, good man!" Win chastised.

I'm not the only one who can hear Win and Arkady. Ironically enough, Whiskey can, too, making life so much easier on me when he takes off on one of his tangents to hunt tennis balls.

"Arkady will get dog untangled—you get the girls some clothes," he directed. "Their lips, they are blue like in Siberia when we do totally naked Russian Spy-

A-Thon." Then he laughed, and just as quickly muffled it when I growled my discontent.

"You do that naked?" Win asked, surprise and awe in his tone. "Kudos to you, bloke."

"You do *not* do this naked in your country, Zero?" Arkady still occasionally slipped and called Win by his old spy name, Zero Below.

"And stick our pasty-white toes into snow? Not on your bloody life, friend."

"Boys!" I warned, my temper flaring. My dream was falling down around me, months of hard work crumbling, and they were reliving Naked Spy Ironman.

Okay, okay, okay. I needed to take a deep breath before I went all *Fight Club*. However this had happened, these people weren't responsible for this assault on my Christmas-loving soul. But they likely had answers as to who did.

Under my breath, I whispered to Win from a clenched jaw, "Would you go find Belfry for me, please? Be sure he's okay. I'll try and get to the bottom of this."

"Of course, Dove. I'll be right here if you need me. Just call."

An inhale in and an exhale out and I shook off my utter horror as a swirl of light-projector ghosts—with their middle fingers in the upright position—whizzed across the front of the house. Deciding the carolers were the closest to me, and least likely to run far, or even very fast in such skimpy outfits, once they saw my rage, I headed straight for them.

Keeping my eyes on their faces, I approached the

group, catching the first pair of eyes willing to gaze into mine—which happened to belong to a very thin young man wearing a Superman Speedo.

His Adam's apple bobbed as his singing warbled and faded off into the night. He gave me a sheepish look when I snatched the ball from the two beach bunnies next to him and lobbed it over their heads. Stilling his brass bell, he gaped at me, waiting.

"You," I said, pointing at him, attempting to keep my voice steady and non-confrontational. "*Why* are you dressed," I waved my hand up and down along his body, "like *this*?"

His lanky body shivered in violent protest, making the bell clang a tinny cry. "Not because I don't need the money, that's for sure."

Rolling my eyes, I planted my hands on my hips. "Listen, I hired you guys to dress like carolers from the eighteen hundreds and sing *Christmas carols*, not sing the playlist from Chubby Buddies Steak and Gentleman's Lounge in your skivvies! Why did you all show up in bathing suits and—and whatever theme this is?" I pointed to another young woman's fishnet stockings. "Where's my 'Joy To The World' and 'I'll Be Home For Christmas'?"

A young woman with lustrous copper hair, also shivering so hard her teeth were chattering, gripped the ties of her bikini top and sighed an exasperated sigh. "Because that's what our boss told us to do. We thought we were dressing as carolers, too. But our boss said there'd been a last-minute change in the work order and we should wear beach party/burlesque attire —as skimpy as possible. We thought it was a crazy combo. I mean, who mixes bikinis and burlesque? But we've done worse in less—it just wasn't this cold. Seriously, do you really think I'd be here in a bikini when it's forty-five degrees out if I knew we were actually going to be doing this outside? Not enough money in the world, lady."

I blinked at her, my shock clear. Someone had changed the work order? "*Who* changed the work order?"

A young girl, maybe no more than college age, pushed her way from behind the others and frowned at me, her raven eyebrows swooshing together as she shook her bell in my face in an angry gesture, her pale fingers trembling with the effort.

"Listen, lady. We're not customer service, okay? We show up and shut up and that's that. Everyone's gotta make a living. Now do you want us to sing another round of Def Leppard or should we move on to 'Walk This Way'?"

I fought a good stomp of my feet and began to pull out my phone, fully prepared to call the Christmas Twenty-Four-Seven people, the place I'd hired the carolers from, when a handful of beads landed on top of my head.

My blood pressure soared upward with a sharp spike. "Hey! Get down from there!" I bellowed up at them, but they couldn't hear me due to the whir of the wind machine, blowing glitter and bubbles.

Without thinking, I ran for the ladder I'd left on the side of the porch for any last-minute technical emergencies and climbed up the rungs to the second floor.

Sticking my pinky and my index finger in my mouth, I tried to get their attention with a sharp whistle. "Ladies! Get down from there now!"

One of them actually smiled coquettishly and winked a flirty false eyelash at me, continuing to gyrate to the sounds of the carolers, who had indeed struck up "Walk This Way."

"I said, *get down*!" I hissed, grabbing for the banister as I hiked up my caftan and swung my leg over the wood.

Hopping onto the balcony—there was very little room to move about and even less clothing on the women—I grabbed a handful of beads from one woman in a tight pink leather bustier with a gold zipper and shook my finger at her. "Give me those beads and get down from here!"

"Hey! Knock it off, lady! Didn't anyone ever tell you it pays to be nice to the staff?" A buxom brunette huffed the admonishment from crimson lips.

My head began to beat out a dreadful pound, but that wasn't the worst of it.

The worst of it, Stevie, you ask? But how can it get any worse?

How much worse does it get than an Easter bunny on your roof, spitting Easter eggs from his butt, while ghosts from some hidden projector fly through the air and give you the finger? How much worse does it get than plastic pink flamingos and baby Jesus zombies?

I'll tell you how. It gets worse when the headlights from the Eb Falls van pulls into your driveway and blinds you with the harsh glare of a reminder your judgment day has arrived.

The very van bringing a car full of ten persnickety, matching-blazer-wearing, rule-abiding, seventy-year-old judges who were sure to have the vapors when they laid their judgey eyes on this fiasco.

That's how.

I felt almost as naked as the women surrounding me. In my panic, I wanted to lunge at the side of the house, spread my arms and legs wide in an attempt to cover this debacle and hide my horror.

Whoever had thrown up all over my house with every decoration for every holiday on the calendar had covered every nook and cranny, ensuring there was no hiding this.

One of the women dropped a string of beads over my head with a grin and a tweak of my nose. "Don't look so glum, chum. You're having a party! Let's celebrate!"

Swatting the beads away, I let my head hang between my shoulders in order to gather my wits and a reasonable explanation for the judges, but there was no time to gather anything before a loud screech of dismay sounded when the judges piled out of the van and spilled onto my front lawn.

"What is this abomination?"

29

I closed my eyes and gulped. Mrs. Vanderhelm and her highfalutin' had arrived and I was officially doomed.

So I did the only thing I could do. I hissed one more terse order at the ladies to "put those beads away!" (as if that was going to make everything better. It was like putting a Band-Aid on an open-heart surgical incision) before I swung my leg over the railing and climbed back down the ladder to face my execution squad and take my licks like a man.

As the judges gathered in a semi-circle, their eyes reflecting the residual vomit of the varied holidays displayed across my lawn and all over my house, I waved on a wince. "Evening, esteemed judges! Welcome to…um, my home."

As their eyes swiveled toward me in unison, some shocked, some disgusted, and one or two pair amused, I smoothed my clammy hands over my rumpled caftan, forcing a smile in the very moment another rainstorm of beads showered down from the balcony.

Several of the colorfully-hued plastic necklaces nailed Mrs. Vanderhelm's head and shoulders. "Oooh! *What in the world?*" she squealed and sputtered, stumbling over one of the Styrofoam tombstones, her ankles twisting in an attempt to keep her balance.

"Mrs. Vanderhelm!" I made a valiant short leap forward, almost successfully catching her. Alas, I slipped in a patch of mud and steamrolled into her instead, sliding into an almost split.

Which, of course, knocked Mrs. Vanderhelm to her

knees—you know, where there was plenty of mud to sully her pantyhose.

Bending my knee, I twisted the upper half of my body and planted my palms on the ground so I could dig my heel into the soft earth in order to rise—and slipped again. As in, total face-plant in more mud.

As the male judges hauled a sputtering Mrs. Vanderhelm upward, I spit the grass and dirt from my mouth and wiped my eyes with the sleeve of my caftan, only to be assaulted again with another batch of necklaces.

Looking upward amidst the onslaught of hard plastic falling down around me, I yelled to the women on the balcony, "Hey, you up there in the pink spandex and kitten mules! Did you bring all the beads in New Orleans? How many of those stupid necklaces do you have? Enough with the stinkin' beads!"

"I see you're entertaining our guests, Stevie. I can always count on you," Win teased with a husky chuckle. "Still looking for our man Bel. Will pop back in momentarily. Oh, and do tell the lovely lass in the red string bikini, clinging to the banister for dear life, she mustn't wear that color. It clashes with her skin tone." And then he laughed and his aura disappeared.

On a grunt, I somehow managed to regain my footing, only to find the judges gaping at their tombstones while they muttered angry words and Madge Bledsoe dabbed at Mrs. Vanderhelm's skirt with a tissue.

On a ragged breath, I wiped my filthy paw across my hip and stuck my hand out in the group's general direction. "I'm Stevie Cartwright. Remember me? You know, from all those meetings you had before the big day today? The pleasure's all mine."

But no one took it. In fact, I think Ralph Acres wrinkled his bulbous nose in distaste before driving his hands into the pockets of his trousers and looking down at his feet.

That's when I saw the big multicolored beach ball the carolers had been tossing about catch the wind and clunk Mrs. Abernathy square in her surly face.

She sputtered, flapping her hands and crying out as I ran for the ball and kicked it as hard as my leg would let me, while two of the judges soothed her.

Licking my dry lips, I stuttered, "I can explain, Mrs. Abernathy. Okay, wait. I can't explain. I mean, I have no explanation for how this happened. I—"

"Are those women in their—their *underwear*?" Madge Bledsoe screeched, pointing up to my balcony with a knobby finger.

"Yep, they sure are," Frank Morrison said on a lewd cackle, before Hank Winkowsky nudged him in the shoulder, effectively shushing him.

Blowing a breath from my lips, one that whistled on its way out, I attempted to make a joke. "So I guess the avant-garde approach wasn't the way to go?"

And cue the crickets.

Well, except for Mrs. Vanderhelm. Her lips went thin in her pudgy face even as her eyes, fringed so thick with mascara her lashes looked like spiders' legs, narrowed at me. Her angry gaze made a louder impact than any sonic boom.

Thus, I quickly decided this wasn't the crowd for my improv. So I put on my apologetic face. "If you'll all just let me explain. Here's the thing. I just got home from work and I don't know what happened—"

"And these tombstones? Can you explain why our names are on them? Are you mocking our committee and the contest? A contest that has been a tradition for fifty years in Ebenezer Falls, Miss Cartwright. Or need I remind you?"

I cocked my head at Mrs. Vanderhelm and her question, peering at her in the glow of the red light in an attempt to read her facial expression. "What? *No!* I would never—"

"Wouldn't you, then?" she asked, lifting a penciled-in eyebrow as she tapped her clipboard with her red pen of death. "Wasn't it you, in all your sarcasm, who asked all those questions about whether the stringent rules we take quite seriously for this contest allowed for one to breathe?"

Oh. Okay. Yeah, I had asked that. But they only had a million and two rules, and as Mrs. Vanderhelm had set about the tedious task of reading them aloud, I'd tried to lighten the boredom. Obviously, I needed to learn to read my audience better or shut up, the latter probably being my best bet.

I shot her a guilty look as another stiff breeze ruffled my thin caftan, slicing through the fabric and making my knees quiver.

"I did, but I swear to you, Mrs. Vanderhelm, despite my crass jokes, I took this contest very seriously and I adhered to all the rules. I adhered so hard, I was like Gorilla Glue. Swear it on my secondhand Kenneth Coles. I don't know what or how this happened, and I know this surely means I'm disqualified, but won't you all please let me at least offer you some nourishment for your trouble? Maybe I can find a way to explain this to you. If you'd all just come inside, I have a delicious—"

"What're you gonna feed us in there, arsenic and frog testicles?" Ralph asked, rubbing his round belly on a snort.

Frannie Lincoln's eyes nearly rolled to the back of her head when Ralph said the word "testicles," making Madge and Frank reach for her to keep her from collapsing. Her teased, marshmallow-colored hair flopped in the wind as she backed away from Ralph, swatting at his hands with a pinched expression on her face.

"This is a disgrace, Stevie Cartwright! How could you bring us all the way out here only to laugh in our faces?"

I nodded in her direction, tucking my hair back from my face as the rain began. "Yep. It's a big disgrace, Ms. Lincoln. But if you'll only let me explain, I'll try and make it up to you. I hired Pascal Le June to make you some tasty treats for my open house. You remember him, right? He's the chef who came all the way from France to work for Petula? The one who

34

makes ze pastries lighter than air?" I asked in my sadly lacking French accent.

Pascal had been all the buzz in town when he'd arrived. Everyone wanted to meet him, rub elbows with him, sample his amazing delicacies. My hope was that he and his tempting treats would at the very least keep me from getting kicked out of future contests.

Ah, and then I noticed it looked like I'd caught someone's attention, because Ralph perked up and winked at me. "We can't let the little gal go to all that trouble without at least takin' a peek, can we, folks?" He looked at his fellow judges for confirmation.

"Everyone follow me inside!" I encouraged before they took the opportunity to refuse Ralph. I said a prayer that at the very least, the snacks I'd so carefully picked out were just waiting for the judges to gobble them up.

Blowing up the front porch steps with a finger to my neck, gesturing to the carolers to can it, I was hit with some beads midway, followed by the boisterous giggles of the women on the balcony. "Knock it the fudge off, ladies!" I bellowed upward, fighting my way through cobwebs and plastic spiders.

Gripping the handle of the door, I heard Madge chastise Hank Winkowsky. "You mind your eyes, Hank, or I'll tell Wilma! And what are you lookin' at anyway, Ralph Acres? Isn't that child bride of yours enough to keep your eyeballs in your head?"

"Ralphie's got a trophy wife!" Frank sang.

And that was true enough. Ralph had made quite a

splash earlier this year when he'd married a woman almost thirty-five years younger than him. She was beautiful and tall and most of the ladies in town, especially the soccer/yoga moms, hadn't welcomed her with open arms. But that was just jealousy talking. I thought she was quite lovely.

As Frank teased Ralph, I pushed my way inside on a long groan, crossing my fingers and toes the interior of the house didn't look as bad as the outside.

I almost sighed in relief when the scent of vanilla and rich chocolate reached my nose. *Please let there be festive red and silver platters full of puffy pastry and drizzled with the richest caramel glaze ever, sitting by a roaring fire, strategically placed near the ten-foot Christmas tree I'd climbed a ladder eleventy billion times to decorate. Please,please,please,please,please.*

But my relief was short-lived when I heard a scream from outside. A terrified, bloodcurdling scream.

Now what? Had someone recreated the movie *Saw*? Were there zombies stumbling across my lawn, crying out for brains? Maybe Norman Reedus *had* actually shown up?

I flew back down the steps to see what else had gone wrong, tripping into one of the carolers, our limbs tangling together before we righted ourselves and I saw what the screaming was all about.

I gasped a breath so sharp, my lungs stung.

Aw, c'mon. Really?

For reasons only Mrs. Vanderhelm could explain, probably out of morbid curiosity, she'd meandered over to the vulgar nativity scene, where she now stood with her hand over her mouth as her fellow judges gathered round her in protective formation.

Ah. So that explained where my Joseph had gone. Caught by the garish beam of red light from the balcony, the crown of his smashed papier mâché head was poking out from behind one of my leafless hydrangea bushes. Somehow, in my panic and dismay over the zombie Jesus gnome, I'd missed that.

But that wasn't all I'd missed.

I'd also missed the lifeless body of the famous pastry chef, Pascal Le June.

CHAPTER 3

*U*pon my arrival, and in my sheer horror, I guess I hadn't noticed the lumpy brown tarp under the hydrangea bush. My eyes had been too busy taking in the entirety of my debacle rather than pinpointing the specifics.

The tarp shivered in the ever-growling wind from the Sound, lifting upward then wafting back down to shroud Chef Le June once more. Ralph scurried to pull the plastic sheet away from Pascal's face while Hank knelt next to the chef, his fingers at his wrist, before he bellowed, "Call 9-1-1!"

I skidded to a stop just short of falling into Madge and Mrs. Vanderhelm, who'd huddled together like two sparrows in a hurricane, their spines shivering in their smart judge blazers. Peering over their shoulders, I hissed my disbelief, praying the chef was simply unconscious.

But his slack jaw and glazed-over eyes suggested

otherwise. He wore his typical white chef's uniform, currently spattered in mud and dried grass. There were scratches on his right cheek and both his fists were clenched in tight balls. Huh. Maybe he'd caught one of the bare limbs of my hydrangea bush as he'd fallen? Had there been a scuffle?

Hank clucked his tongue and shook his gray head. "He's gone. Dang shame. Made some mighty fine sweets. Loved those things with the hard pink shells."

Ralph pulled a handkerchief from the inside of his jacket pocket. "Aw, yeah. And those marmalade-filled things. Whaddya call 'em again?"

"Petite fours, isn't it?" Hank wondered aloud.

"Dove! Is that...? *Chef Le June?*" Win squawked the question.

Closing my eyes, I gave a silent nod before I placed my hands on both Madge's and Mrs. Vanderhelm's shoulders. "Please come inside while we wait for the police, ladies. You can wash up and get warm. You're both going to catch your death—"

Mrs. Vanderhelm stiffened with an appalled gasp, tucking her plaid handbag against her side in a defensive move.

Sighing, I corrected my poor word choice. "I mean a cold. Please, ladies." I turned to the rest of the judges to convey my sincere invitation. "All of you, in fact. Come inside while we wait for the police to arrive. It's warmer, and I promise no frog testicles."

Now Madge gasped, too, but even in his shock, Hank still snickered. Using slight pressure, I steered the two judges toward the house then gave them a light nudge.

As the group turned and began to make their way inside, their voices filled with fear, I scoured the area where Chef Le June laid, my eyes squinting when the red light from the balcony made another pass across his body.

How had I missed seeing him there? I felt awful about it.

"*Nyet*, my succulent petunia! Not another murder?" Arkady whispered with marvel in his tone.

I winced and squatted on my haunches, angling my head to get a closer look at Pascal, taking in the strong, almost too sharp angles of his paling face. Honestly, he was in insanely good shape for someone who'd spent the better part of their days creating flaky crusts and custard cream-filled confections.

His skin was stretched taut over his cheekbones, the scratches on them infinitely more defined as a result. His wide eyes—a deep green, and the talk of all the ladies in town, single or otherwise—stared in blank repose beneath bushy but well-kept raven eyebrows.

"Stevie?" Arkady prompted for an answer to his question.

I shrugged in confusion. Mostly, there was nothing to see. "I don't know what happened, Arkady."

And I really didn't. There were no signs of any obvious blunt trauma, no blood to speak of other than the drying scratches on his cheek, no gunshot wounds (thank heaven). Though, there was a bit of something crackled and glistening at the left side of his mouth.

Crumbs from one of his delicacies? He prided himself on taste-testing every batch of pastries he made.

Which begged the question, what the heck had happened? Chef Le June wasn't even supposed to be here tonight. He didn't do "ze menial labor," according to him. He'd made that very clear when I'd hired him.

When we'd first met, he'd very arrogantly informed me his confections were on display, not him. I vaguely recall him saying he was no horse and pony show, or something like that, while Petula giggled at his awkward English metaphors.

The plan had been to have one of Petula's staff arrive at our house just a half hour shy of the time I arrived home to prepare for the judges. That person would set everything up and be on their merry way. The delicious scent of coffee brewing meant someone had at least been here. In fact, Enzo, our contractor/friend, had been instructed to let Petula's staff member in before he left, with the promise they'd lock up on their way out.

But then I remembered, the front door hadn't been locked...

Belfry!

I froze, my chest tightening. "Has anyone found Belfry yet? Is he okay?"

"No, Dove. Not a sign of him anywhere. I've looked all over the house, in his favorite plants in your bathroom, the backyard, which is utterly absurd, considering our good man's penchant for the heat. I even looked in the vase by the fireplace, his latest favorite naptime haunt."

I heard the slight panic in Win's voice, the concern. I knew my Spy Guy pretty well now. Okay, there were exceptions to that statement. I still didn't know how even *he* hadn't known he'd been adopted and had a shady twin brother who'd threatened to steal everything from us. In life, he had worked as a spy for MI6, for gracious sakes. You'd think it would be a given he'd have all his loose life ends tied up.

I also didn't know much about his ex-girlfriend, Miranda. The woman he was convinced had killed him, and a beautiful, mysterious fellow spy.

But I did know his tone of voice. I knew when he was giving me upper-crust British disdain because I loved fried Twinkies and Pop-Tarts. I knew when he was mocking me simply to mock for his own amusement, and I knew concern. So his words were like a punch to my gut, one almost so real, I had to poke my fingers into my ribs to keep my stomach from losing its lunch.

I bolted upright, pressing my knuckles into my temples. "You couldn't find him." I spoke the words aloud in order to process them.

"Not anywhere, Stevie. But I'm certain he's about. You know our Bel. He's a crafty bugger. Likely, he's found some new place to nap we just haven't come upon yet."

"You two, go inside and make pretty with the sour-puss-face judges," Arkady ordered. "I, Arkady Bagrov, like all good Russian spies, will search for my comrade Belfry until the soles of my feet bleed. Go now before they become suspicious!"

Turning away from Chef Le June's body, I moved back toward the house, trying to keep my panic at bay. I almost didn't care about the scream of sirens or the shock of the judges. I only knew I had to find Belfry.

Something was wrong. Something was horribly wrong.

As my hand met the door handle once again, the blur of activity around me still in full tilt, I had a premonition about Bel. Just like back in the day when I'd still been a full-fledged witch.

The kind of premonition a witch feels when her familiar is too far from her, when the invisible thread of their tether is broken.

"Stevie? What's happening? Talk to me, Dove."

Shaking my head, I fought tears and whispered, "Something's wrong. I know something's wrong. Bel's missing and it's not good, but I don't know why, Win. I don't know what's happening. I haven't had a premonition this strong since I lost my powers."

"Your powers?" a voice from behind said. One I recognized, and had even come to welcome. Well, except in times like these, when there was a body in the middle of my lawn and I was sure to end up grilled with questions like some steak at a barbecue.

Fighting to keep my emotions in check, reminding

myself Bel was notorious for hiding out during naptime, I forced a smile and turned to one of my very favorite officers of the law. "Yippee. Officer By The Book's here."

Officer Nelson shot me a quick smile, his skillful policeman's scowl breaking before he resumed his usual resting-stern-face position. "What about your powers, Miss Cartwright?"

I flapped a dirty hand at him and his crisp uniform with the perfectly straight trouser lines. "Oh, you and your overly sensitive policeman-like hearing must be on the fritz today. I didn't say powers, Goof. I said flowers. As in, there's a body in mine. And are we back to calling me Miss Cartwright again? I thought we'd moved past that two crime scenes ago?"

Clearing his throat, he gazed down at me in all his rigid handsomeness and winked before straightening his already impeccable posture. "I'm on duty."

We'd been through a thing or two, Officer Nelson and I, including the death of his girlfriend, Sophia, this past summer, and one murderous romp through a cemetery, wherein I'd saved his life. Nowadays, we occasionally shared a cup of coffee in the mornings before he headed off to his shift and I opened the store.

Don't get me wrong, I was still that nosy nag of an amateur sleuth who was forever bugging him for information about open cases and getting in over my head in matters I shouldn't. But since he'd lost Sophia, I was less naggy, more friend.

And I liked it that way. Dana was a grand, honest

soul, as pure as they came, and while we still played this game of pretentious formality, I knew deep down he liked me a little, and probably much to his dismay.

I reached for the set of beads caught around the badge on his chest and held them up into the flashing lights of the ghosts still swirling on the front of my house. "I see you've met the ladies?"

Planting his hands on his hips, Officer Nelson sighed the sigh of the beleaguered. "I know there's an awkward, totally outrageous explanation for them, Miss Cartwright. I'm every bit pins and needles, waiting to hear it."

We both stopped and cocked our heads when a strangled, warbling noise from behind my front door interrupted our conversation. Our eyes met as if to ask, "Am I hearing things?" But then we shook our heads in dismissive unison and smirked at one another.

Nah. No way.

"Holy cats! What the heck's goin' on around here, Stevie?" Sandwich, my second favorite Eb Falls police officer, shouted as he pounded up the stairs, drowning everything else out.

I rolled my eyes and shrugged my shoulders. "Why, whatever do you mean, Sandwich? Everything's right as rain."

Large and beefy, with shortly cropped dark hair, my gentle giant frowned down at me. "Didn't you enter the Christmas Lights Display Contest? What gives with the Easter bunny on the roof and the ladies and gents in, er...their underwear?" he asked, pointing to the bare legs of the carolers, who'd now stopped singing and had closed ranks, snuggling against one another in their retrieved coats.

"Uh, yep. I sure did enter. I went all out, too. But you know what I think is really gonna cinch the deal? The half-naked carolers singing Def Leppard. What say you, Sandwich?"

He paused, assessing me just as another sparkler from the demented Uncle Sam on the porch flared up. "Oh. Sarcasm. I get it. So what happened here? Where are all those decorations you kept talking about? And what happened with Chef Le June? Did you see anything?"

My answer was cut off when someone inside my house screamed. Though, this was a much different scream than Mrs. Vanderhelm's. It was a little drawn out, rather piercing, and maybe even a little more terrified.

Officer Nelson brushed past me, driving the heel of his hand against the door to push it open fully.

The judges were positioned in a half-circle at the base of my staircase, their eyes wide, their mouths open. I followed their line of vision to the top of the steps, where a skittering-scratching noise dragged my focus upward. And then it happened.

In fact, a whole flock happened.

Turkeys, that is. Yep. That's right. The *sound* Officer Nelson and I heard on the porch moments ago had, in fact, been turkeys. An entire flock of them (more than two is a flock, isn't it?), waddling into the sitting room at the top of the stairs, overlooking Puget Sound.

"Miss Cartwright?" Officer Nelson and his "how will you explain this one?" tone asked.

With that question, the turkeys began dropping downward, pecking and gobbling in low squalls, their clawed feet beating out a frantic rhythm while they paced from step to step. They were obviously as stunned as we were, judging by the surprised blinks of their beady eyes.

Frannie Lincoln squealed in alarm, throwing herself at Frank Morrison and wrapping her legs around his waist. She clung to his neck in fear, her aging hands clenched behind his head. "I hate birds!" she cried, burying her face in Frank's neck.

"Shooooo!" Mrs. Abernathy screeched, flapping her purse at them as they continued to advance.

"Stevie!" Sandwich shouted, rushing the stairs to herd the turkeys as their gobbling grew louder. "What's going on?"

Yet, I could do nothing more than blink in my own surprise. I had turkeys in my sitting room. Someone had put not one, but *four* turkeys in my house. What in the name of Pete was happening? Then I realized, it was the amount of turkeys pecking their way down the stairs that troubled me.

Four. There were four of them.

That's when it hit me. I'd ordered four turkeys total from Gobble Unlimited. One for our personal Christmas feast, and three for donation to the church for the Eb Falls Christmas Eve party. That was no coincidence, was it?

As the turkeys rambled about, their gobbles growing louder, their necks bobbing and dipping, I stood transfixed.

Win's abrupt shout of an order roused me in my discombobulated state. "Dove, snap out of it and take control. The detectives have arrived!"

With a shake of my head, I attempted to clear my mind of all the questions I had about turkeys and baby Jesus imposters and sprang into action. "Sandwich! Herd those gobblers back up into the stairwell and down the hall to the guest bedroom on the left! Judges? Follow me into the parlor, please, so we can all be in the same place to greet the detectives." Turning my voice to the open door, I yelled, "Half-naked carolers and naughty ladies, get in here and warm up!"

The moment the words escaped my mouth, I caught sight of Detective Sean Moore behind the crowd of people pushing their way into my house. Dressed as per usual in low-slung jeans and a T-shirt beneath his dark brown blazer, his rippled muscles flexed and tensed as he took my front steps two at a time.

Since this past summer, when his partner, Detective Ward Montgomery, murdered Officer Nelson's girlfriend, Sophia, in a paid-for-hire mob hit then attempted to murder me, Sean Moore had been on his own. While the Eb Falls Police Department searched for a replacement, I've seen a bit of a transformation in

Detective Moore since his time without Detective Ward.

Oh, he was still pretty snarly and cocky, but those attributes were currently tinged with a new humbleness I'd never witnessed to this point.

Rumor around Eb Falls was he blamed himself for not catching on to Detective Montgomery's extracurricular activities for the mob. I'd heard Officer Nelson mention that particular revelation to Sandwich. Dana said it had brought a whole new dynamic to Detective Moore's investigations nowadays. He was more careful, more thorough, and more empathetic.

Unfortunately, it didn't bring a new dynamic to *our* relationship.

He still didn't like me overly much and I can't say exactly why—other than we'd originally met under interrogation-like circumstances, and I'd met his cocky with my own brand of cocky and our two cockies had collided.

Regardless, he'd likely be lead detective on this one. But then I saw someone behind him. Someone short and curvy with copper-red hair in a messy bun atop her head, held in place by a funky-colored headband.

She wore a green T-shirt that read Dunder Mifflin (which made me send her a silent thumbs-up. I loved *The Office*) beneath a cropped leather jacket with spikes around the cuffs and along the wide lapels. Her jeans were loose and looked comfortable, her high-top sneakers pink and green.

She smiled at me from behind a glowering Detective Moore and waved cheerfully. "You're Stevie Cartwright, yeah?" she asked, holding out a hand with a multitude of rings.

I wasn't sure if it was a good thing or a bad thing that she knew my name. But I gave her a half-smile in return while taking her hand and giving it a quick pump. "That's me."

She grinned even wider, her eyes shiny and brown "So cool! I'm Melba. Er, Melba Kaepernick... Um, I mean *Detective* Melba Kaepernick. Shoot. I'm still getting used to that title. Anyway, you're the lady who talks to dead people, right? So-so cool! I've heard a gazillion things about you since I joined Eb Falls PD a few weeks ago."

I eyed Detective Moore—who looked rather pained at this point—with a raised eyebrow. I was sure she'd heard plenty about me from him.

"I bet every last one of those gazillion things was complimentary, too."

"Well, no. Not all of them. In fact, most of them weren't very nice at all, but I like to judge for myself—"

"Detective Kaepernick?" Detective Moore ground out, gripping Melba's upper arm. "We have a dead man outside. This isn't a social call. And there are witnesses inside. Go do your job and talk to them. You know, make like a real detective?"

"Sure-sure," she agreed on a nod as she disentangled her arm from Detective Moore's grip, her eyes narrowing ever so slightly in his direction before she caught herself. Then she turned back to me, her smile back in place. "Anyway, super to meet you. Totally wanna grab your ear in the near future—"

"Kaepernick!" Detective Moore groused. "*Go!*"

Melba scurried past me and into the parlor where the judges had gathered, as Detective Moore glared at me.

"Not just a new partner, but a brand-new detective, too, Starsky?" I teased, referring to one of the many TV cop names I'd called him and his ex-partner. "Your world must be all kinds of turned upside down."

He made a face and clenched his angular jaw. "Uh, yeah. Fresh-off-the-truck detective."

I wagged my finger at him. "Serves you right for gossiping about me, Starsky. I've helped way more than I've hindered—"

"Pascal!" a voice shrieked from my lawn. "Pascal, where are you, *ma cheri!*"

Petula, our local caterer, pushed her way past people and Detective Moore, tears streaming from her swollen eyes. She grabbed my arm, her hands ice cold. "Stevie, is it true?"

My heart crashed against my ribs. I hated this part. Hated it so much. I liked Petula a lot. She was our go-to for any event Win and I hosted. Though, I will admit, the whole Pascal thing never felt quite right. But seriously. What did I know about true love?

I'd been dumped at the altar by my ex-fiancé Warren and I'd had absolutely no idea he was cheating on me when he did the dumping. To make matters worse, I was a witch at the time. You'd think my

Spidey-witch senses would have picked up his cheater's vibe. Love really can make you turn a deaf ear.

So I pulled her into a tight hug and squeezed. "I'm so sorry, Petula. Please, come inside and I'll get you something warm to drink while we figure this out, okay?"

But she shrugged me off, her red-rimmed eyes wild as the wind tore at her hair. "No! I don't need anything warm to drink. I know who did this, Stevie! I know who killed my sweet Pascal!"

CHAPTER 4

J gripped the edge of the sink in my guest bathroom after washing my hands and throwing cold water on my face, a little overwhelmed from the flurry of activity outside the door.

"Win?" I called out, catching the ugly truth of my appearance in the mirror. I looked pale and tired, with deep purple smudges beneath my eyes. Oh, and muddy. Very muddy. "Win? It's okay. I've finished up." We had a strict rule about my private time—that included the bathroom. Win never went past the threshold of the bathroom unless I called to him.

My Spy Guy's warm aura wrapped around me in a gentle hug. "Dove. Oh, Dove, what can I do to comfort you while they finish up out there?"

"We need to figure out what happened to Belfry, Win. Where could he be?" As per Detective Moore, I wasn't allowed to leave until everyone was questioned. But that didn't help me where Bel was concerned. I couldn't look for him while on lockdown. Time was of the essence here—maybe even crucial.

Why did I feel in my gut time was crucial?

"I'll confess, I'm at my wit's end about now, Stephania. Whiskey's going absolutely mad upstairs, pacing back and forth like a bloody caged tiger while Arkady attempts to soothe him and the turkeys. You know how he gets when he's away from our man Bel for too long. But I've looked in every cranny of this house we call home, and I've come up dry. It's as though he's fallen off the face of the planet."

My stomach clenched into a tight knot—so tight I had to sit down on the toilet seat. "I can't feel him anymore, Win. I don't know what to do about it. I can almost always feel him, but there's this hole now. This big, empty hole and...and..."

I bit back a sob and focused on the framed picture of some cliffs in Ireland by an artist Win had found while we'd antiqued. I had to remain calm. Nothing would be accomplished by losing my mind.

"I know, Dove. I know. Please, let's just concentrate on getting everyone out of here so we can begin a proper, unencumbered search. Tell me about Petula. What in all of heaven did she mean when she said she knew who killed Pascal? Has this been labeled a murder already?"

I shook my head. "No. No one's said a word about that, but Petula's convinced Pascal's wife is responsible."

Win gasped in clear outrage. "His wife? The

scoundrel! Has he been wooing our Petula whilst in the confines of marriage?"

Swallowing hard, I clenched my fists tight. "No. Not exactly. According to Petula, he's separated from his wife—whom, according to Detective Kaepernick, still lives in France."

"And how accurate is that assessment?"

"I don't know. The detectives are looking into it as they question everyone, checking airlines and customs. But we have more than just Chef Le June's death on our hands, Win. We have turkeys, and Easter bunnies, and baby Jesus zombies. What in the world is going on? Who did this, and how could they have possibly switched out all my decorations in such record time? I mean, how much time between Petula's staff arriving and Enzo leaving does that give a person to pull off something of this magnitude?"

"That's a good point. Clearly one needing investigating. We must ask Enzo if the egg-dispensing Easter bunny was on the roof when he left, and we need to find out who Petula sent to do the setup. Also suspicious? The number of turkeys now lounging about in our guest bedroom, soiling the one-hundred-dollar-a-square-yard, oyster-white carpet. There are four. Upon recollection of your order with Gobble Unlimited, you ordered four turkeys, did you not?"

My misery deepened. "I noticed that, too. But maybe it's just a coincidence? Maybe we're just being overly observant?"

"No, Dove. I don't believe that—especially not if we

both took note of that fact. This is all connected. I firmly believe this madness is also connected to Bel's disappearance. There's not a chance in Purgatory Bel would have allowed this sort of nonsense, had he been present. Someone is toying with us, and I want to know *whom*."

Shivering, I remembered my conversation with the "Pour Some Sugar On Me" singers. "One of the carolers said their boss told them the work order had changed at the last minute, and if everyone would just get out of this house, we could call them and ask who they spoke with!"

"Dove, you're panicking. I hear it in your voice. I feel it. Please, I beg of you, attempt calm. I know how dearly you love Belfry. We all do. But it will do no good if we don't do what we do best to try to find him."

"Sleuth."

"Indeed."

Then something dawned on me. "Do you think...do you think it was Balthazar who did this?"

Of course! Win's evil twin!

I knew Win's voice would be filled with snappish tension before he even spoke. Balthazar was the sorest of subjects for him.

"As we've discovered since he, too, disappeared into the great unknown last summer, he's quite incompetent, Stephania. He couldn't even pull off showing up to steal all our money. It was rather in the bag for him, wouldn't you agree? I'm dead. He's not. He has my DNA. He had a test to prove as such. Yet, when the

56

time came to hornswoggle our riches, he was a no-show. How could he possibly do something of this magnitude if he couldn't show up for a simple meeting?"

That was a fair statement. It was true, Balthazar had shown up here in Eb Falls, slick as the day is long, posturing and gloating about how he was the real Crispin Alistair Winterbottom and how he was going to take every last penny of Win's riches from me. But the very day we were to meet with our mutual lawyers, the meeting was cancelled and no one had heard from him since.

Further investigation did, in fact, prove Win and Balthazar were separated at birth and given up for adoption. Balthazar went into foster care for most of his life, and Win went to the woman who, though now deceased, he still lovingly calls mother.

The more I thought about it, the more true the theory rang. "But you have to admit, he does have motive. He hates my guts. He hates yours, too, even though he's never laid eyes on you. I'm telling you, he harbors serious resentment that you weren't tied up in the foster care system. You had a home. A family. He was jealous. How he got his hands on all your pertinent background information, I don't know if we'll ever know. I mean, you're a spy and even *you* didn't know you had a twin or that you were adopted, for goodness sake."

"I think the point here is," Win said in a dry tone, "I didn't know I *needed* to look for anything, Stevie.

Clearly, Balthazar wanted to locate his family because he didn't have one. I had one. One that kept things from me, but one nonetheless."

I winced. This was the sorest subject ever. I hated venturing into these waters, but Bel was on the line and a chef was dead. "Still, looking back on his smug conversations with me, he was definitely jealous of how you'd landed, where your adoption was concerned. That's motive enough for me."

"I still don't know what to say about my alleged adoption..." Win muttered, making my heart tug.

When we'd found out Balthazar really was Win's identical twin, and we'd done some serious digging, we'd come up with an adoption agency called Hopeful Horizons based in London. So we'd snooped, and then we'd snooped some more via all manner of totally illegal avenues.

Yes, I said *illegal*.

I don't care that we chose some shady ways to go about finding out where Win and Balthazar came from, and that's just the honest truth. Sue me. I simply couldn't bear dejected, lost-without-answers Win. He'd been so blindsided after finding out the woman who'd raised him wasn't his biological mother and he'd never had a single clue, I'd vowed right then and there to help him. I wanted to hold his hand during what I'm sure was a painful journey for him—much in the way he'd held my hand when I'd found out my father was alive.

We still hadn't figured out why his mother never told him. Her deception had to have a valid reason, of that I'm positive, because according to my International Man of Mystery, he'd had a pretty happy childhood. So what had Win's mom been hiding, and why?

"I'm sorry, Win. I don't like bringing him up. I know how much finding out something like that hurt you. But it's still a viable explanation."

"Then why didn't he show up to that meeting, Stevie? He could have had it all."

"No. That's not true. MI6 has your fingerprints and they were willing to hand them over to prove you were deceased. Balthazar might have your DNA, but he can't have your fingerprints, Win. Maybe he got wind of the fact that we were going to force him to give up his fingerprints, got scared off and flew the coop."

"Bah! Fingerprints are easily faked."

I rolled my eyes, bracing my hands on the tops of my thighs. "When you're an International Man of Intrigue and work for MI6—maybe. But not when you're an average kid raised in foster care who worked at a cell phone store before he found out about you."

"All that aside, it's not a reason to sabotage your Christmas decorations, Dove. Not to this extent."

I pushed all my fears about Bel aside and tried to focus on getting everyone out of my house so we could physically search for him. "Okay, so let's set your evil twin aside for the moment. We still have a saboteur. Someone made the outside of our house look like a brothel, and there's a reason. I just don't know what it is. We also have a dead chef on our hands. One I'm praying wasn't murdered."

"Maybe he had a heart attack, Stevie? It certainly wouldn't shock me. He did spend his days indulging in gooey pastries."

"He's in pretty great shape for a heart attack, but stranger things have been known to happen. I'd bet there are plenty of folks who look like they're in perfect health on the outside, but inside lurks hardening arteries or high blood pressure. I hate to say it, but if he had to die, I'd rather they declared something of that nature. We've had a lot of murder lately, Win. After Sophia last summer…" I stopped, swallowing hard. Sophia's death was still the hardest of all our murder investigations combined. "I guess I'm still feeling pretty sad about her."

Win's mournful sigh shuddered in my ear. "I mirror that sentiment, Dove."

A sharp rap of knuckles on the bathroom door forced me to stand up. "Miss Cartwright? You're needed out here."

"Dove?"

"Mmm?"

"I'm here. I'm right here."

My insides warmed. There was no disputing that fact. Win was always with me. "Thanks, Win," I whispered as I popped open the door to find Officer Nelson with his arms stoically crossed over his broad chest.

"Where to, Officer Happy Pants?" I asked.

Dana actually snorted. "That's a new one."

I chuckled. "But is it your favorite one?"

"Nah. I'm still pretty partial to Officer By The Book. It's neck and neck with Officer Rigid. Anyway, now that you know my kryptonite, mind talking about your idea of Christmas decorations? I don't get it, Stevie. Were you going for some sort of out-of-the-box theme? Because I have to tell you, the tombstones with the committee names on them? Quite the personal touch."

As he asked the question, I stopped midstride and looked around. Whoever had thrown up all over the outside of my house hadn't bothered with the inside. There was still a touch of Christmas in every corner.

From the pearl lights strung through pine boughs with red and silver Christmas ornaments atop our kitchen cabinets, to the sprigs of fresh holly and ivy on one surface or another, my joy hadn't totally been stolen.

I stopped just outside the parlor door, where everyone had gathered for questioning, and gave him a glare. "I had absolutely nothing to do with that. I know it's a hard answer to swallow, considering the obvious care someone took in pranking me, but when I left here this morning, it was Christmas all day long. So while we investigate what happened to Chef Le June, how about we also consider I've been vandalized, and maybe the person who did this has something to do with what happened to the chef?"

Officer Nelson tapped my arm, stopping me from entering the fray of my noisy parlor where my enormous Christmas tree sat, glowing and perfect, surrounded by bikinis and stiletto heels.

"You're telling me someone switched out your decorations for the witch with the wand in her... Well, you know."

I jabbed at the air with an angry finger. "That's exactly what I'm telling you, Officer Rigid. In the eight or so hours I was gone, someone, probably someone who thought I might give them a little competition, made that mess out there. I'm sure they're rolling around just laughing and laughing about it as we speak. But right now, we have a death on our hands. So for the moment, let's go and get this handled. We can talk about the cretin who ruined my entry in the competition later."

He motioned for me to enter, rolling his arm in a grand gesture. "Sounds like a plan. After you, She Who Talks To The Dead."

Now I snorted. "Nice improv, Officer. Very nice."

"Two can play your game, Miss Cartwright," he said on a smug chuckle before directing me to the group Officer Moore was in the process of questioning.

When my turn came, and Sean Moore only shot two or three less-than-snarling questions at me then dismissed me, I have to say, I was stunned. I wasn't sure if he hadn't grilled me like our days gone by because he thought I was now a trusted witness to a crime, or he was just done with me in general because I got under his skin.

Either way, I decided to go to the back of the line

and simply observe as I fought to keep from screaming at everyone to get out of my house so I could search for my familiar.

While I waited behind Petula and some of the carolers, I finally had the chance to give a good look around and see if indeed Petula's staff member had placed the pastries where I'd asked.

Sure enough, they were exactly where I'd requested —on a gorgeous antique buffet right next to the fireplace, highlighted by the glow of our Christmas tree.

A mound of delicate, fluffy squares sat upon a silver tray, glistening with colored sugar. The secret-recipe salted-caramel sauce Chef Le June had bragged so over—in a matching silver server with ladle—was right next to them, on a Sterno in order to keep it warm.

The cookies in various shapes and sizes, hand-painted with some sort of fancy technique, were there, too, along with ten dainty coffee cups, one for each judge.

But right now, with Bel missing, all those fancy confections were nothing more than possible clues to the circumstances surrounding Chef Le June's death and my familiar's disappearance.

That made me spring back into action. I placed a light, supportive hand on Petula's shoulder and gripped. "Can I get you anything, Petula? Coffee? Tea, maybe?"

She turned to me, her rounded cheeks red as she smoothed her wiry hair back from her face. "I can't believe he's dead, Stevie. If it wasn't his wife, who would do this?"

Reaching for her hand, I gripped it and shook my head in compassion. "I don't know, Petula. What made you think it was murder?"

Her lips thinned into a smeared red line of lipstick. "Because his wife threatened to kill him, Stevie! I heard her on the phone with him one night. I know I shouldn't have been eavesdropping, but I…"

Aha. He was a cheater. That was definitely a motive for murder. Affairs of the heart always were. "But you were in love with him, right?"

Petula nodded, letting her chin fall to her chest. "Yes, and he was in love with me. He told me so," she stated, defiance in her tone.

"Did you know Pascal had a wife, Petula?" I'll admit, I waited with bated breath to hear the answer. I'd be upset if she'd begun an affair with a married man, but I also understood the power of a man's appeal all too well.

Her grip on my hand tightened as her lips quivered. "I didn't. I swear I had no idea. When I found out and confronted him, he swore to me they'd been separated for over a year and once he met me, he'd asked her for a divorce. That was exactly why she threatened to kill him. He told me he didn't tell me about her because he was ashamed he'd ever married her."

I didn't like what I was hearing. I didn't like it one bit that Chef Le June hadn't told Petula he was otherwise bound legally to another. Nothing good ever came of beginning a relationship with a lie. Not to mention, it was dang suspicious.

"Did he tell you she was actually threatening him because he told her about the two of you, or are you just putting two and two together? Did you discuss the phone call he had with his wife?"

Now she looked disgusted, as though I'd asked her a ridiculous question. Her cheeks went crimson and her eyes narrowed at me. "Of course we did! I'm not an idiot!"

Instantly I gripped her hand harder while we moved up in the line of people waiting to speak to the detectives. "No, Petula. I would never think that. I'm just trying to help. Promise."

Then she crumpled against me and began to sob. "I know, Stevie. I'm sorry. I'm just on edge is all. I don't even understand why he was here at your house to begin with."

My Spidey senses—you know, the ones I lacked where my cheating ex was concerned—stood at attention. "I wondered that, too. I thought one of your staff was coming to set up?"

"That was the plan. Edmund was supposed to bring everything by, set it all up, then move on to the mayor's Christmas party directly after."

"And where's Edmund now? Did you try to contact him?"

"I've tried and tried, just like Detective Kaepernick asked, but his phone just rings and rings. It doesn't even go to voice mail, and he's not at the mayor's party.

No one's seen him since he left the shop this afternoon."

How odd. "Did he leave with my pastries in hand?"

Pulling a tissue from the pocket of her oversized sweater, she sniffled into it and shook her head. "I can't get any confirmation one way or the other, Stevie. So far, no one remembers Edmund even leaving, but the pastries that were in the cooler labeled yours are definitely gone. I swear, I don't know what's going on!"

Her voice began to rise, which was my cue to ease up. Tucking her arm under mine, I stroked her wrist. "It's okay, Petula. Take some deep breaths."

"Will you stay with me when the detective questions me?" she asked, her voice trembling.

I smiled in sympathy, pulling her even closer. "Of course I will. I'll stay right here. That's a promise." I rested my chin atop her head and sighed, still trying to keep my misery over Belfry in check and in perspective.

That's when I saw something tucked under the platter holding the pastries. Something that looked like a note. "Hang on one second, Petula. I'll be right back."

Setting her from me, I picked my way through the judges, their eyes flaring with accusation as I excused myself toward the table by the fireplace hearth and cocked my head.

Upon inspection, there was a note scrawled on what looked like Petula's letterhead from her store. I wrapped a cloth napkin around my fingers and lifted the platter.

I bit back my gasp of shock when I read:

Dear Stevie, I made this opera cake especially for you. I hope you will take a moment to enjoy your hard work before your esteemed guests arrive.

Bon appetite!

Chef Pascal Le June

Dropping the platter back into place, I noted a foreign-looking pastry with a bite missing, on the very top of the mound. One I was sure I hadn't ordered from the chef. Cut into a rectangle, the treat had layer upon layer of chocolate and some sort of puff pastry. A sprinkle of sugar completed the package of perfection.

It truly was beautiful, a feast for the eyes. In fact, I couldn't take my eyes off it, the sugar sprinkled over the top virtually danced across the surface, mesmerizing me.

The sugar.

Hadn't Chef Le June had something around his mouth—something I'd thought was crumbs from his pastries—or had I been seeing things? Why would he make a pastry just for me? In fact, why would he care if I relaxed before the judges arrived?

Sure, I'd made it clear I needed everything to be perfect, but Chef Le June wasn't exactly aware of much but himself. He'd barely spoken to me when I'd placed the order other than to tout his many accomplishments, before he'd whisked off to Petula's kitchen in flagrant fashion.

Yet, now he was making me special pastries and

telling me to put my feet up? And who'd taken a bite out of my dang pastry?

Just then, Ralph Acres sidled up to me and gave me a nudge with his shoulder. "These look delicious and I'm starving. Your decorating might stink to high heaven, Stevie, but your food looks pretty darn good. Too bad it doesn't count for your overall score," he said, reaching for the opera cake.

I froze, my mind a whir of buzzing thoughts.

What had looked like crumbs on Chef Le June's mouth, plus a specially made pastry just for me from one of the most self-absorbed men I'd ever met, plus a sugary-sweet note, plus a dead chef out on my lawn, equaled...

"Mr. Acres, nooooo!" I shouted, knocking the pastry from his hands and startling him.

Ralph fumbled trying to keep his hold on the cake, his pudgy hands reaching out as he began to back away and instead tripped over my artfully placed carved reindeer.

He lost his balance then, a slow motion sort of thing where I grappled to reach for him, to keep him from falling, and couldn't seem to get a good grasp. Ralph wide-eyed with surprise, his body in a constant fumbling-backward motion.

"Ralph! Look out, old man!" Frank Morrison yelped from across the room where he stood with Detective Kaepernick.

But it was a little too late. Just as I managed to get my hand around his wrist, he jerked it backward and toppled all the way, his bulky body a blur of judge's blazer and orthopedic shoes, felled as though cut down by a lumberjack.

Right into the Christmas tree.

Branches flopped and twisted, the lights I'd spent four hours stringing in a teardrop pattern ripped from their comfortable nest of pine, and ornaments rained down everywhere, crashing to the floor in unison with Ralph.

I crashed, too. Directly on top of him like some sumo wrestler with a clunky body-slam move.

CHAPTER 5

"*I*'m so sorry, Mr. Acres!" I repeated for the millionth time as the paramedics loaded him onto a gurney, tucking him safely into place.

He lifted his double chin and looked up at me with watery eyes. "I just wanted something to eat, Stevie. We've been here forever and I missed supper," he moaned out, his misery etched in the lines on his face. "Now look what happened."

As Ralph had fallen backward, I'd grabbed for him, but he'd tried to shake me off, and we'd ended up colliding in the worst of ways. In fact, I'd probably helped tip him backward. Add to that, I certainly hadn't made anything better by landing on top of him.

He'd made for a great cushion for me. However, the reverse wasn't true for him. Ralph had somehow twisted his leg in such a way that he'd fallen on it at an awkward angle. Just thinking about that visual, when

I'd scrambled off him and looked down at his crumpled form, made me want to cry.

Oh, this was so bad. So, so bad. Yet, I plowed onward with my apologies and reassurances as everyone continued to mill about my parlor, stepping over broken branches and shattered ornaments.

I latched onto his hand and held it tight. "I'll pay for everything. I promise. You won't have to worry about a penny of your hospital bill. Not a single one."

"You broke his leg, Twinkle Toes. How about you let him get that taken care of before you break something else?" Detective Moore muttered in my ear, his sarcasm burning my already testy britches.

My temper flared with a white-hot spike. "Oh, you hush, Starsky. It was an accident! Why don't you go do your job and get those pastries to a lab to have them tested and don't let anyone touch them, because I'm going to bet those devilish morsels are the culprit in Chef Le June's death!"

Everyone still in the room stopped what they were doing and gasped, staring at me with distaste for a moment before they clearly realized it was just Stevie Cartwright theorizing, and returned to gathering their things to make their way out.

Detective Kaepernick plucked a piece of tree from my hair and held it up with an interested glance. "What do you mean the pastries are the culprit? We don't even know what happened to the chef yet. How do *you* know what happened?"

As she asked me the question, her eyes never left my

face, but they weren't hard and accusatory. They were thoughtful and inquisitive.

I could certainly see why she might have great success getting people to trust her. Her openness, as opposed to Detective Moore's snarling, growling act, was undoubtedly refreshing.

Running a hand through my mud-flecked hair, I sighed. "Call it a hunch. Call it intuition. Call it whatever you like, but when I saw Chef Le June...er, in my garden, I caught a glimpse of something around the corner of his mouth. Something I thought looked like crumbs—which made sense. He always taste-tested his food. But as you already know, he wasn't even supposed to be here today. That alone is suspicious to me. In hindsight, and after reading that note he allegedly left me, whatever was at the corner of his mouth looked exactly like what was on top of that opera cake. Which is why I tried to prevent Ralph from eating it. So, it only makes sense to consider the pastry could be involved in this, don't you think? The hitch in this giddyup is what's got me stumped. Why would he make a pastry for *me* then eat it himself? If *he* didn't bite into it, who did? Then there's this to consider—if it turns out the pastry is poisoned, who wants to poison *me?*" I shivered a little. Did someone want to poison me?

Melba held up her hand. "Don't get too far ahead of yourself just yet, Miss Cartwright. Those are all valid theories, but we don't even know what happened to the chef at this point. Sure, I don't know why he'd take a bite out of a cake he made for you, there could be a ton o' reasons. But we can't jump to any conclusions before we have some evidence. You know that better than anyone, right?"

That was fair. I did know that. But I had a bad feeling anyway. Still, I went along with her by smiling and nodding. "I'm just doing what I do and theorizing. It's a habit I can't seem to break."

Detective Kaepernick leaned into me as though we were sharing a secret. "Yep-yep. Gotcha." She scribbled on her small notepad and nodded.

"Don't forget to note the particularly unusual nature of Chef Foo-Foo Wahoo's generous gift and his charming letter," Win encouraged. Clearly, he'd noted how odd the letter from the chef was, too.

There was that to take into consideration, too.

"Also, something to think about while you're writing things down. Chef Le June was…" I paused, hoping to keep my voice low and my next statement diplomatic, in light of Petula's apparent love for Pascal. "Well, he was a little self-absorbed. For him to leave me a note as warm as that, and a specially made pastry on top of it is…unlikely. I'd have the note not just tested for fingerprints, but I'd also have the handwriting analyzed and compared to Chef Le June's. And don't forget the bite out of the pastry. It should be compared to the chef's dental records. "

Sean Moore made his stern face at me. I'd seen it before. It was the expression he used when repri-manding me and my penchant for supposition and interference. "Well, look at our fledgling detective throw around orders, would ya? I know exactly where you're going, but this hasn't been labeled anything yet, Miss Cartwright. You don't even know if it's a crime scene yet. Right now, it's just a death. So, I'm warning you to tread lightly and let us do our job."

Wrinkling my nose, I sighed. Always with the resistance to my theorizing. I just don't get it. "I'm only trying to help, Detective Moore. I have been right a time or *four*."

"*Four*?" Melba Kaepernick crowed. She held up her fist to me. "Niiice! Girl power, right?"

I bumped her fist in return and smiled. "Well, the first time was just a brush with death. I didn't actually figure that one out. So I guess it's only three and a half. He did try to kill me, though. That should count for something on my resume, don't you think?"

Of course, I was referring to Winterbottom's cousin Sal. Shortly after Spy Guy and I met and made that crazy pact to find Madam Zoltar's killer, we'd discovered Sal thought he was going to inherit all Win's riches—not some lowly, unemployed ex-witch like me. When he found out otherwise, well, let's just say he tried to kill me.

Gosh, that felt like such a long time ago. Yet, it had only happened in the beginning of February. Here we are, ten months gone by, one house renovation, a rescue dog, more bumps and bruises than a prize-fighter, and four murders later, and I couldn't imagine my life without Win.

Detective Moore rolled his eyes and sucked at his teeth. "Where'd we be if you weren't giving us direction, Miss Cartwright? Lost. That's where. Like little lambs in the big scary woods. Hey, when did you graduate from the academy again?"

"Lay off her, Moore," Sandwich said, his beefy arms tucking an escaped turkey to his side. "Chief sent word to wrap this up. So let's do it. You have any more questions for Stevie? Or can we call this a done deal? She's got a heck of a mess to clean up and we have a ton of reports to file."

Sean Moore flapped a hand at me in a dismissive gesture, tucking his notepad into the inner pocket of his blazer. "Yeah, yeah. We're done here. But don't fly the coop," he ordered then laughed at his joke.

"Coops are for chickens, Starsky. You'd know that if you read a book instead of watching all that *Naked and Afraid*! Just because it's on The Discovery Channel doesn't mean you can label it educational!" I yelled at his retreating back, infuriated.

Sandwich stroked the turkey's head in a soothing manner and gave me his apologetic face. "Sorry, Stevie. I don't know how this little guy got out. They're gettin' a little stir-crazy up there."

"It's okay, Sandwich. I don't even know why I have turkeys to begin with." This still puzzled me no end.

"I was afraid to ask. In fact, I'm not going to ask because that's a whole can o' worms I'm just not up to tonight. But listen, I can take at least three of them if you want. I know a guy who owns a farm down the way a bit. Gave him a call after I herded them upstairs. His granddaughter loves the little buggers. Believe it or not, they make good pets. Anyway, he said he'd take 'em in for sure. At least until you figure out where they belong. But he can only take the females. One in your group is male, and their mating season's right around the corner."

I wasn't sure I wanted to know how Sandwich knew a turkey's gender or its mating rituals, but then terror struck my heart. I know this comes off as completely crazy, but it's one thing to see a turkey in the frozen food section of your grocery store, quite another to look at their little faces and realize they're destined for someone's holiday table.

My love for animals and my love for turkey smothered in rich gravy with some stuffing on the side are always at war with one another. I stroked the back of the turkey's head and winced.

"He won't... I mean, I know it's silly, but this farmer friend, he doesn't raise them to..."

Sandwich grinned, his round face going cheerful. "Eat 'em? Aw, heck no. Promise. They'll be safe and sound. He's got lots of land where they can roam free. He actually grows corn, so no worries."

I patted his arm in gratitude. "Thanks, Sandwich. I appreciate this. I owe you one, and thanks for saving me from Detective Moore."

"Now if only you could save *me*," Detective Kaepernick muttered with a frown before her face filled with guilt. "Sorry. That was inappropriate."

I began using the toe of my shoe to push ornament fragments into a pile. "Hah! Don't be silly. You're entitled to not like your new partner. He's still bruised from his last one and all his secret mob dealings. That makes him cranky, I'm sure. I think he's pretty upset because he never once caught on. No one did. The fact that *I* did was pure luck."

"Yeahhh," Melba drawled. "He mighta mentioned that. Hey, maybe if you gave us a funny name? Maybe that'll help him lighten up. You know, like Beckett and Castle—Caskett?"

As much as I liked Melba Kaepernick, and as much as I sympathized with her having to partner up with Sean Moore, I needed to get everyone out of our house so we could find Belfry.

"How about I give that some thought and get back to you?"

She gave my shoulder a playful nudge with her fist. "I'd feel a lot more like I was part of the team if you did. I hear when you give someone a nickname, it means they're in the club."

Despite my worries and the disaster area my house had turned into, I laughed out loud. "The club? I'm pretty sure I'm the only member of that club. Haven't the guys in the department warned you about me? I drive them bananas."

"Aw, for sure. But I've heard a few of 'em talking when they thought no one else was listening. There's a lot of respect there, Miss Cartwright. They might not like it, but I heard them say you're pretty good at solving a murder."

"Well, look at you, Stephania. Respect from your peers is quite admirable indeed. Even if they're still in the closet about it." Win crowed his approval.

My cheeks went hot, but my spine straightened at the compliment. "That's really nice to hear. I really don't interfere to be a pest. Though, I'm sure Starsky would disagree. I genuinely only want to help, and sometimes I get carried away."

Melba smiled wide, her bright eyes picking up the glow of the only remaining Christmas lights left draped on the fireplace mantel. "I heard that, too. Which is why I'd like a nickname. Maybe the guys will be more accepting. I'm pretty far from home. Miss my family. It'd be nice to at least have something to joke about with the guys at the station."

My heart clenched. How could anyone resist this adorable, fresh-faced woman? I sure couldn't. She was a refreshing change from Growly Pants Moore. But I had to for now. I needed to get on with the search for Bel.

"Men can be such territorial goons sometimes. Forget them and tell me where you're from. I detect a slight accent."

Those bright eyes of hers fell to her feet. "A really small town in Maine."

I looped my arm through Melba's and began directing her over the mess of the parlor floor and toward the front door. "I knew I heard a bit of an accent! Wow. You really went to the extreme, coming to this side of the country, didn't you? Either way, welcome to Ebenezer Falls. Drop by anytime. Maybe for lunch? My door's always open here and at the store."

"That's really nice, Miss Cartwright. Thank you. I'd better get back now. I'm sure the station's a hornet's nest."

She sounded reluctant to leave and torn about her reluctance. I sensed Melba loved her job but wasn't a fan of the newb syndrome—or the way the all-male Eb Falls Police Department was treating her. I wondered why she'd left Maine, but that question was for another time.

My head bobbed and I smiled. "You bet. Please tell Starsky if he has any more questions to give me a ring-a-ling."

The dark night swallowed up her hearty laughter as she made her way back down the front porch steps. I closed the door and clenched my eyes shut with a deep inhale.

"Are we ready to begin, Dove?"

I made a break for the stairs, hiking up my caftan's hem, taking the steps two at a time. "Let me check on Whiskey and our remaining turkey guest and then we'll hit this."

Even as I said the words, my stomach tilted and churned. Something was very wrong with Bel's disappearance. I just couldn't get a feel for *what* was wrong because it *all* felt wrong, and as I raced down the hall to check on the turkey and Whiskey, I had to keep my legs moving or I'd sit down and cry.

～

*L*eaning on my elbows, I watched the turkey peck at the wood flooring in our kitchen, fighting the hot sting of tears.

"No, no, my *malutka*. Do not cry. I promise you, we will find our little ball of cotton candy if I have to turn your America inside out! I am good spy. Zero is good spy. We will be good spies together. Double the spies. This I promise you."

We'd retraced every single step Win had taken when he'd first hunted for Bel. Then we'd done it all over again. An hour later and Bel was nowhere to be found, Whiskey was miserable without his best buddy, and I had a new turkey friend who was surprisingly easygoing, considering all his other friends were now on a farm in a heated hut.

Whiskey moaned at my feet. He'd stopped pacing, but his sheer misery resonated in every deep sigh he took. I reached down and scratched his ears, loving the velvet feel of them, before I sat up straight, determined to find my Belfry.

Wiping at my tears, I clapped my hands on my legs. "Okay, so let's treat this like we would any other investigation. First, I think we should contact the company who hired the carolers. They must've spoken to Bel. How else can we explain the change made from Victorian-era singers to beach bunnies and leather? But then we have to ask ourselves, why would Bel do something so awful? He wouldn't. You guys know it. I know it. That means it had to be someone else. Maybe someone pretending to be Bel? Which still makes no sense. They'd have to know the name Bel uses when he does any kind of business transaction for us."

"Good idea, Dove. Then we must call the establishment where you purchased the turkeys. I find it highly suspicious you had four turkeys roaming the house and that very number matches the order you placed. You did order four turkeys, didn't you?"

"Yeah. Yeah, I sure did," I mumbled with a wince. "Which would lead one to believe switching out live turkeys for the kind you find in the frozen food section is some sort of literal twist to this elaborate joke? I also ordered pigs in a blanket. So what's next? Real pigs wearing blankets?" Immediately, I frowned. "Oooo, forget I said that!"

"Speaking of turkeys, throw Strike here some leftovers. Surely we have oatmeal or some cereal. He's likely starving, the poor gent. It will keep him busy as we make calls."

As I grabbed my phone, I frowned when Win's words sunk into my brain. "*Strike?*"

"Well, of course I mean the turkey, Stevie."

"I don't get it."

"As in the term used in bowling, Stephania. Surely you know if you throw three strikes in a row it's called a turkey?"

I learned something new every day about my Spy Guy. "Did you do something as small town and mundane as bowl when you were alive, Win?"

His amused laughter was rich. "I did indeed. I'm quite the bowler, in fact. I was once a teenager, too, Stevie. I wasn't always a super spy who traveled the world and romanced beautiful women as easily as some put on their socks each morn."

As I scrolled through my phone to find the number of the nice young gentleman in customer service who had helped me choose the actors to play the carolers, I went to the cabinet and stuck my head in to see if we had any oatmeal.

"So he has a name now?"

Strike followed behind me, brushing my thigh, his feathers rustling against the fabric of my jeans as he pressed his head into my leg. I had to admit, he was incredibly affectionate and terribly sweet.

"Of course he has a name. A name and no home. What are we to do whilst we look for a home for him? Throw him out in the cold? Leave him nameless and hungry? It's Christmas, Stephania. Surely we'll house him until we figure out what to do with him."

I don't know that I truly knew the depth of Win's compassion and generosity. Each time I thought I'd reached the bottom of his well, he went deeper.

Pulling out a box of oatmeal, I ripped it open and scattered some on the floor. Strike instantly made a dash for it, pecking and clucking low, making me almost smile.

"I would never throw a helpless animal out in the street, Win. Of course he stays until we find better digs. In the meantime, I'll call Christmas Twenty-Four-Seven and find out what we can about our carolers."

Scanning my phone, I located the name Chuck, the customer service rep I'd first spoken to when I'd begun hatching my plan to sweep the town Christmas Lights Display Contest.

As the phone's shrill ring droned in my ear, I sorted my thoughts until I heard, "Christmas Twenty-Four-Seven, this is Chuck speaking. How may I make your holiday spirit shine brighter?"

"Chuck? Stevie Cartwright here—"

"Ah! Miss Cartwright! I hope you're calling to tell me how satisfied you were with our service. As in five-out-of-five-stars satisfied? If you'd just click on the link to our website and take our customer survey—"

"Chuck! I am not satisfied!" Panic fueled my tone, and I knew it, but my nerves were raw with Bel missing for almost four hours now and Chuck's tone was too bright, too animated and too full of good cheer.

There was a small pause, a hiss of breath, and then Chuck was back on his feet again. "Oh no! I'm so sorry to hear that, Miss Cartwright! How can we make this right?"

"First, Chuck, you can tell me how the heck my work order was changed from Victorian-era carolers to women in bikinis and bustiers, singing Def Leppard and Aerosmith?"

I heard the furious clicking of a keyboard, and then Chuck—sunny, pleasant, unflappable Chuck—squawked, "*Bikinis?* Heavens to Betsy! How did this happen? We talked for almost an hour when you placed the original order and I remember you specifically said you wanted actors who could not only sing and play bells, but they must be dressed in Victorian-era garb. I don't understand, but I'm looking up your order as we speak and…"

There was a small gasp even customer-service-provider-extraordinaire Chuck couldn't hide before he exhaled.

"And?" I prompted.

"Well, Miss Cartwright, it's right here. It says someone called this morning and changed the order…"

"*Who* called this morning, Chuck?" I gripped the phone tighter.

"Your virtual assistant, Miss Cartwright. Yes, here it is, right here. One Bell Fry, from Connecticut."

"Did you take the call, Chuck?"

"No, Miss Cartwright. Unfortunately, I was detained. My mother and a big ugly corn on her toe took up the better part of my morning at the podiatrist. Though, I will admit, it's awfully strange the customer service agent who *did* take the call didn't make mention of such an enormous change. I'm the senior customer service rep on this account, after all." He paused then, and spoke the next words as though he were reading them and they hadn't quite sunk in. "However, there's a notation on the account, and I'll admit once again, it's rather odd..."

My internal alarm bells rang loud and clear. "What does the notation say?"

"Oh, sweet Destiny's Child!" Chuck squealed, the attempt to keep his tone calm long gone. "It says 'the more skin showing the better'. Right here on my screen in big bold letters, Miss Cartwright! That doesn't sound at all like you or Mr. Fry!"

No. It sure doesn't.

"*Bell Fry?*" Win's question whistled in my ear. "That's Bel's code name. The one he uses when he does all of our Madam Zoltar business, too. Someone is toying with us, Stephania."

Win was correct. Bel would never do something like that. Which could only mean someone knew his code name...knew far more about us—me—than they should. Knowing an intimate detail like that meant whoever had pulled off this prank had very private information about us. No one but the three of us knew Bel used that made-up name to represent himself as my virtual assistant whenever we had phone or Internet business to do.

"Miss Cartwright? Are you still there? I'm sending a text to my supervisor as we speak. I'll get to the bottom of this if it's the last thing I do. You can take that to the bank and they will suffer my wrath. Oooh, will they suffer. Of that I assure you!"

I swallowed hard and began to pace the length of the kitchen, the palms of my hands breaking out into a clammy sweat of rising trepidation. "Thank you, Chuck. Please, as soon as you have any more information, give me a call. Use this number when you do."

I clicked the phone off before I screamed, my heart thrashing against my ribs as I reached for the edge of the countertop and clung to it until my knuckles turned white.

The silence of the room pounded in my ears, the stillness of the house without Bel zipping about drove his absence into my very soul. My gut was right. I knew I was right. This Christmas debacle had to do with Belfry's disappearance.

"Boss!"

When I'd told Win earlier I couldn't feel Bel anymore, I'd meant it. But just as earlier I'd felt the distinct lack of his presence in my heart like a dead weight, that very presence rushed right back in, making my chest swell in an almost painful wave.

"Boss! Help me!"

CHAPTER 6

"*W*in, Arkady!" I whisper-yelled. "Did you hear that?"

"Arkady Bagrov hears nothing, my *malutka*."

"Dove? What is it? Talk to us."

Holding my finger up to my mouth, I silently shushed them and cocked an ear to the room.

"Steeeeeevie! Help me!"

My heart shifted and clenched. He was afraid. Wherever Bel was, he was scared. I heard it in his tone. "Bel! *Where are you?*"

"Boss! Help!" Bel called out, the last word beginning to fade and warble.

"Belfry! Tell me where you are!" I cried, my eyes scanning the kitchen as though he might appear out of nowhere—which, by the by, was ridiculous. Bel didn't have magic. He couldn't appear and disappear at will.

"Has she lost, as the Americans say, her marbles, Zero?" Arkady asked, his question clearly hesitant "Sit, my sweet potato. You must sit and rest. You are hearing things."

"No!" I yelped with a shake of my head as I ran from the kitchen toward the front door. "Bel is out there— somewhere. I hear him, Arkady! If I can hear him, surely the two of you can!"

"Dove! I hear nothing. Nothing at all. Talk to me, Stevie! What is he saying?"

Maybe only I could hear Bel because he was my familiar? But did that mean... No. No. I refused to believe he wasn't of this Earth. Besides, if he were on the other side, Arkady and Win would be able to hear him. Wouldn't they?

I didn't know anymore. Since I'd become a human, the rules had all changed. I wasn't supposed to be able to hear ghosts since I'd lost my powers. Yet, I heard Win and Arkady as though they stood right in the room with me.

But so far, I'd only heard a couple of other spirits from the afterlife without assistance from my spies, and the instances had been very random. Still, none of this made any sense.

"*Beeeel!*" I bellowed again, yanking open the front door to look out into the night sky. But the only thing that greeted me was the harsh glare of that ugly red light and the littered mess of my front lawn.

I ran out onto the front porch and peered into the darkness, leaning over the railing as the pelt of a hard rain pummeled my face. "Belfry, answer me! Please!"

Win's warmth encompassed me, beckoned me.

"Dove, come back inside. You're frightening Whiskey—and me, for that matter. Please come inside and let's talk this out."

But I brushed Win off as I headed back inside, closing the door behind me. Maybe it was because this particular mystery involved one of the most important people in my life, or maybe it was because I was a bigger amateur than I thought, but I didn't want to talk anything out, even as I knew that was exactly how we'd figure this out.

Climbing over the debris in the entryway, I headed for the kitchen and some coffee. "I can't think straight, Win! Bel needs me. He called for me. He said he needed help. Why can't you and Arkady hear him?"

"I don't know. I only know we must continue to piece this together. That means we next call the establishment where you ordered your turkeys, and we keep asking questions and inquiring until we find our man Belfry. Now snap out of this, Stephania, and focus!"

"Zero, don't be so hard on our girl. She is like sparrow—fragile. We don't want to break her tiny wings."

Summoning up another breath of air, I sucked in as much as possible before I held up a hand in protest. "No. He's right, Arkady. I'm not at all my most logical because this is Bel we're talking about here. But Win is spot on. I need to keep calling everyone involved in the making of this nightmare. There's a connection we're not seeing here. Bel is out there…somewhere. I heard him. That wasn't my anxiety playing tricks on me, and it all goes back to whoever sabotaged the decorations and changed the carolers."

"Here's something else to consider, Dove. If in fact this connects to Belfry, it has to have something to do with magical foul play, wouldn't you agree?"

I blinked and stopped short of reaching for the coffeepot as Strike pecked at my feet. "How so?"

"Enzo, Stephania. Think about the time frame. If Enzo truly did leave just after Chef Le June arrived, who would have enough time to take down the Christmas decorations that took you almost an entire month to put up if there weren't magic involved? As I recall, the plan was for you to arrive shortly after both Enzo and someone from Petula's staff left. It's simply not *humanly* possible to have redecorated the entire house in that amount of time without the use of some sort of magic."

My mouth fell open and my stomach turned. "Do you think…?"

As I considered Win's words, my head swirled. My Spy Guy was right. There was no way, even with a crew of people, someone could have done all that damage outside in that short amount of time.

Could Adam Westfield, the warlock responsible for literally slapping the witch out of me, be the one who'd done this? But why would he kill Chef Le June?

And then another horrible thought crossed my mind. If Adam was responsible for Chef Le June's death, had he killed him from the afterlife like he'd tried to kill me?

Arkady cleared his throat. "Please, do not take offense when I ask. This magic you speak of so often. Arkady has trouble to understand. You were *real* witch? With wand, and broom, and spells? Like, poof and bippity-boppity-boo?"

My mouth was too dry to answer, so Win filled in the blanks for me. I'd never really told Arkady my history in any great detail, and he'd never pushed for information beyond what he'd heard us occasionally discuss.

He'd never once questioned the idea Belfry could talk either. He'd just taken us all at face value, and I guess, because he talks to the living and he's dead, those facts have cleared up all doubt about the paranormal's true existence.

Still, hearing us discuss this as a possible motive for not only Bel's disappearance, but the Great Christmas Decoration Fiasco of 2016, had to be unnerving—even for someone as tough as our Russian spy, who'd proudly declared he'd seen more interrogations via water-board torture and finger hacking than ten spies see in their careers combined.

Arkady gasped in his dramatic way when Win finished explaining. "You are real witch? My pungent dill pickle is—is magic?"

I couldn't help but chuckle at Arkady's disbelief. "Was. I *was* a real witch with magic. Now I'm just a human. It was more like *Practical Magic/Hocus Pocus* witch than fairy godmother/Cinderella, but that's neither here nor there anymore. And hey, mister, aren't you a dead guy talking to a human? Or is this all nothing but a dream, Arkady?"

"Hah! You make my ribs tickle with your funny. Now you call turkey people and you ask questions while Zero finishes tall tale."

Picking my phone back up, my head a bit clearer now, I scrolled my contacts to find Gobble Unlimited and hoped they had the answer.

While in hushed tones, Win explained the last bit of my history to Arkady, the night I'd lost my powers to Adam Westfield's vengeance, I prayed Harvey was still at his desk. A glance at the microwave oven told me it was almost ten o' clock, but I dialed anyway because if nothing else, I'd leave Harvey a message.

"Gobble Unlimited, this is Harvey, speaking gobble, gobble, gobble, can I help turn your ho-hum turkey into an explosion of dancing flavors on your tongue?"

Pinching my temple, I kept my voice calm even though I was surprised. "Harvey, I'm so relieved you're still there!" Thank heavens for overachievers.

"Is that you, Miss Cartwright? Shouldn't you be enjoying the fruits of your labor right now? As I recall, someone was very exited to enter their neighborhood Christmas decorating contest. Wasn't that tonight? How did that go?"

I almost laughed out loud at how ludicrous the fruits of my labor sounded about now. My laborious fruits were crushed as sure as someone had run my fruit truck right over with a big rig.

"Harvey, I have to ask you a question. Did the order

I placed with you last month go through? You know, four turkeys between twenty and twenty-five pounds? One Cajun-seasoned, three traditional, supposed to be delivered in a couple of days for the utmost in freshness?"

I heard his chair creak as I assumed he leaned back into the seat. "Looks like the order was cancelled yesterday, Miss Cartwright, by a guy named Bell Fry. Said he was your virtual assistant and your plans had changed. He caught our FedEx guy just in time, too. He was also pretty agreeable about the restocking fee, according to the note on your account. You do realize why we have to charge for the restocking fee, don't you?"

No. I didn't. How could you restock a perishable item? But at this point I didn't really care. Yet, a thought struck me then. "Did he say why we were cancelling on such short notice?"

"Yep. Yes, ma'am, he did. He said he cancelled because there was going to be a death in the family. Which is sort of a scary thing to say, don't you think?"

~

I sat immobilized after I hung up with Harvey. My fingers were like the very icicles someone had stolen from my Christmas decorations on the peaks of the house.

"You heard what he said, didn't you, Win? Harvey claims Bel said there was going to be a death in the family and that's why the order was cancelled. As if he knew someone was going to die? Or *is* going to die?"

Win blew out a long breath. "Stevie, I need you to remain calm here. Whoever's up to this monkey business is clearly toying with you. The only death was Chef Le June's. He's not a family member. I realize that's little solace, but it's something."

"Which could mean the person impersonating Belfry knew Chef Le June was going to die?" I almost couldn't comprehend the idea his death was premeditated.

"Quite possibly true," Win offered.

"So Chef Le June's death was premeditated? Harvey said the person who called did so this morning. What's the connection with my Christmas decorations and holiday dinner plans to Pascal? Maybe I'm just too torn up over Bel to see it, but I'm missing something."

"Christmas!" Arkady blurted. "I have feeling on my insides this is right."

I stared blankly off into the kitchen. Yes, all the things happening had to do with Christmas, but I was missing the message being sent, if there was a message at all.

"*Christmas?*"

"I'm with Stephania, old friend. Do explain yourself."

"*Dah, malutka*! You talk, talk, talk about Christmas since summer. You plan for months for the lights, the food, the special pastries from fancy-pants chef. You make things with fire and metal. You spend hours on the phone to make things perfect, you make charts, you draw diagrams better than any spy strategist Arkady knows. And during all this time where you talk, talk, talk, you say one thing, 'This will be best Christmas ever.'"

Both Win and I gasped in unison as the light bulbs above our heads shone. "Someone's out to ruin my Christmas? Is that what we're saying here?"

"*Dah!*" Arkady exclaimed.

Sweet Pete, that made perfect sense—the longer I chewed on it, the clearer it became. But what about Bel? "What does that have to do with Bel's disappearance, Arkady?"

"Will your Christmas not be in the ashes like Chernobyl if our bat friend is not here with you to celebrate?"

"He's right, Dove! That makes absolute sense. Now, what we must ask ourselves is this: Who else could possibly know about Belfry but your witch people?"

My head began to spin, my throat going dry once more. Win was right. No one knew about Belfry but he and Arkady and the people in my coven. Which led me right back to the idea Adam Westfield was responsible for this.

Certainly he was capable of lurking from the afterlife, listening to my plans, putting this all together in an effort to continue to punish me for his death.

"But wait. There's still Chef Le June. He's a stumbling block to that theory, isn't he? What does killing *him* do to my Christmas?"

"My tender lamb chop? I now know you are too close to this investigation because you are not thinking outside this box you American's talk so much about. If the fancy chef is dead when your judges arrive and they cannot dine on his lighter-than-air pastries—"

"It ruins your perfect Christmas!" Win interjected. "Of course, Dove! Whoever is doing this knows how much you wanted to win the Christmas Lights Display Contest. Surely, with all the work you put into decorating the house, and judging by the pictures of past entries, you would have won hands down. I don't doubt that for a second. But there's no chance you'll win now. Chef Le June ending up dead in the middle of your nativity scene certainly, and without qualm, cinches the deal and qualifies as Christmas ruined."

"Yes!" Arkady barked. "Yes! Zero hits head with nail!"

"Hammer. I've hit the nail on the head with a hammer, Brethren In The Spy," Win teased.

"Hammer, head, nail. All used for torture. I mix them up. What I am saying to you is all of these things add up to one big thing and now we must locate the big thing and pull his teeth out with the wire cutters! I will show you how, buttercup. We practice on enemies first, yes? Maybe that scrunchy-face Mrs. Vanderhelm? She would make good first run."

"Oh, Arkady! I could kiss you!" I shouted, whirling in a circle. "All of that totally fits. And no dental work on anyone—hear me? That's not how we roll."

"You are sometimes wet sheet," Arkady complained, but I heard the laughter in his voice.

My adrenaline kicked in with a rush as I began to pace once more, with Strike hot on my heels. "So it's a theme then? Trash Stevie Cartwright's best Christmas ever by kidnapping her familiar and leaving a dead guy on her front lawn? The only person capable of switching out those decorations with magic, who hates me enough to go to all this trouble, is you-know-who."

"Who is this who?" Arkady asked, concern in his voice.

"Adam Westfield." Win confirmed my worst fears.

I almost never said Adam's name. In my mind, it was like saying Beetlejuice or calling up Bloody Mary in your mirror (which is a bunch of bunk, by the by). Speaking his name was akin to putting the hold he had on me out into the ether and giving it power.

"The man-witch who hit our dumpling and took her power?"

I nodded on a gulp. If Adam's responsible, he's sustaining his power for very long periods of time. It's one thing to attempt to take me out on my front lawn (yep. That happened) by zapping me with some lightning bolts, but to have stayed on this plane long enough to do this much damage meant he was even more dangerous than ever before.

"The one and only. But here's something to think about, why would he actually kill Chef Le June? Not to mention, *how*? He tried nailing me with some lightning bolts when he tried to kill me, if you'll recall. It sure didn't look like our chef was fried."

"How quickly we forget my possession of that scoundrel I must legally call brother, Stevie," Win reminded me.

Possession!

Now my eyes went wide as I remembered when Win had possessed his brother's unconscious body—for one mere moment. The memory was bittersweet and made my eyes sting with tears. Win had kissed me that day, and we'd virtually avoided talking about it since.

But then my chest grew tight with the horror of Adam doing the same thing; the endless havoc he could wreak with that ability left me floored.

"How did you do that, Win? It can't be an easy feat. In fact, I've heard of very few real cases of possession, and definitely not one that goes on for an extended period of time." Which is what Adam would need to do to pull all this off—a lot of time on this plane in someone else's body.

"Through sheer grit and determination. That's all I have to offer, Stephania. I suppose you could say I willed it so. I have told you all along I believe I can get back to your plane, haven't I?"

Oh, he definitely had, and I didn't doubt for a minute it took more grit and iron will than most of us possess, but Win's tone suggested he didn't want to talk about his motives for possessing his brother's body.

In fact, he used the same tone just now as he had

when we'd discussed his former love and fellow spy, Miranda. That meant, *subject closed, Stephania. Please don't dig around in my manhood.*

"Wait. Say this once more. You possess body? Down there with Stevie?" Arkady squealed.

Win's laughter tickled my eardrum. "I did, my good man. I suppose that trumps your silly coup in Batswana in 2006, no?"

Oh, no. This wasn't going to turn into an "I'm a more resourceful, tougher spy than you" contest. I'd been to that rodeo, and it could go on for hours as they traded their men-of-intrigue adventures while trying to one-up each other with their ghoulish spy tales.

That conversation would escalate and turn into a fight to the finish for Best Possession of A Body 2016, and heaven only knows I can't chase after two egotistical dead spies while they body hop.

"Gentleman, this isn't the time to pound your spy chests. First, Win was only able to possess his brother's body for mere moments. If Adam is that powerful—powerful enough to possess a body for a long period of time and make someone kidnap Bel and commit murder—we have huge trouble. The consequences are enormous. But furthermore, why would he kill Chef Le June? To what end? Just to dump him in my nativity scene and cause a bigger ruckus? He did plenty just by switching out my decorations and changing orders. Chef Le June isn't someone I hold near and dear like Belfry. I mean, of course I didn't want him dead. But to murder him? That needs a stronger motive than ruining my Christmas, I should think. It feels extreme even for Adam."

Arkady grumbled, which meant he was pondering. "Possibly this dirty man-witch wanted the police to blame you for his murder? Put together with the disappearance of our Belfry and this would most definitely make mess of your perfect Christmas, *dah?*"

The impact of that statement stung my heart as surely as if someone had pierced it with an arrow.

Yes. *Dah.*

Bel was the only friend I'd had to share the holidays with. For many, many years it had just been the two of us, and whatever we could afford to spare on my small salary.

Christmas would never be Christmas without Belfry. Not ever.

And yes, that would make every Christmas forever after a horrible memory. But there was one more theory that hit me like a ton of bricks.

What if ruining my Christmas meant killing me?

That would certainly put a damper on things, wouldn't it?

CHAPTER 7

"*A*ll this talk of ruining Christmas and we've forgotten one thing…"

"And that is, Dove?"

"We're forgetting that note Chef Le June allegedly left for me. That pastry could have been meant for me. Me dead would definitely ruin my Christmas—like forever. We don't know why Pascal was here in the first place. That bit of this still makes no sense. But why would the chef bite into a pastry meant for me if *he* wrote a note telling me how he made *me* a special treat?"

"Ahhh. I think we have theory number two," Win murmured. "Though, it still has its holes.

"I do not like this theory," Arkady grumbled.

I struggled to contain the tremble of my fingers. "It's no secret Adam wants me dead as revenge for his death, guys. It makes perfect sense he'd try and poison me."

"So what we're saying here is he possessed Pascal, made an irresistible treat for you laced with poison and wrote you a note to entice you to eat it?" Win asked.

"Then why does cheating chef eat cake?"

My head was beginning to spin with this missing link. "Okay, okay. Definitely a stumbling block. The fly in our ointment is Pascal—poisoned pastry or not."

"*Dah.* Let us stick to Arkady Bagrov's theory. He was framing you for murder. I do not like the other theory."

"Then let's stay on track and call the next person on our list," Win encouraged, though his voice had tinges of concern I heard loud and clear.

My theory made the most sense.

Setting aside the absolute black void of emptiness I was feeling about Belfry's absence, I fought to stay on track as I dialed Enzo's number. "Okay, if we stick to Arkady's theory about framing me for murder, that means Adam is lurking and listening to our conversations, right? Or sending someone to do his dirty work and report back about our comings and goings. But he'd know I'm the least likely person they police would suspect after all the crimes we've actually helped the Eb Falls police solve. That aside, he'd need some kind of irrefutable proof to frame me, and by the looks of the spot where the chef was dumped, there's not much to go on. Not that I saw anyway."

"Framing conspiracies aside, I would interject with, we don't even know Chef Le June was actually murdered," Win stated. "We have no proof the two incidents are directly related, other than the best-Christmas-ever connection. I suppose we have to wait until they do the autopsy and inspect the crime scene with a more careful eye. There could be footprints, or DNA on the chef's body we don't even know about. Of course, I reiterate, that's contingent upon this actually being a murder, Stephania."

I rolled my eyes and waved my hands like cheer-leader pom-poms. "Earlier you were all gooo murder. Now you suddenly sound like me? What gives International Man of Mystery?"

"I'm simply being cautious like you, Dove. We don't have all the facts on the chef's death. Until such, we let that portion of our dilemma sit and begin asking questions of the people who might have been here when Chef Le June arrived and connect that time with Belfry's disappearance."

Enzo's cell phone went to voice mail, and his wife Carmella was out of town until Christmas Eve. I had five days' worth of casseroles and lasagna in my refrigerator she'd made for me just before she'd left to prove it, so there was no point in trying to call her either.

I traced the pattern of veins on the kitchen countertop with a finger as I put together what Win was suggesting. "So I guess the only thing we can do is pinpoint a time frame for exactly when Bel went missing?"

"Precisely. For all we know, Enzo heard something

—a strange noise, a thump—something that would give us an idea as to the time Belfry disappeared. What could be an enormous lead for us might mean absolutely nothing to Enzo. Certainly, when Enzo makes mention of the strange noises he hears around here, you've poo-pooed him and chalked it up to the house settling or the wind from the Sound. But we both know it's really Belfry puttering around upstairs with Whiskey."

That was correct. I'd covered for Bel at least a hundred times since Enzo had come into our lives. "Oh, and then there's Edmund, too...maybe he heard something off? Did either of you hear if they ever located Edmund? Last I heard, he was supposed to drop off the pastries here then head to the mayor's Christmas party, but no one had heard from him since."

"I believe that's where we left things," Win assured in the tone he reserved for soothing me. "For now, you must rest, Dove. You'll be good to no one, least of all Bel, if you don't at least try and rest your eyes. It's late, and clearly Enzo isn't answering his phone. So come, leave all this until tomorrow. Forget the mess; it can be cleaned up at a later date. Come to the parlor and we'll put The Hallmark Channel on. That always soothes you, yes?"

I began to protest by raising a hand. No sleep until we found Belfry. How could either of my hardcore spies even consider it? But Arkady intervened with an objection much the same as Win's.

"Winterbutt is right. You must recharge brain. If you are not sharp and do not have wits about you, mistakes will happen. We cannot have mistake for our Belfry's sake, *malutka*. You must only take on that which you can control. You can control your state of mind and not make things worse. When even the best spy is tired, he lets his emotions get best of him."

They were right. I couldn't let my emotions get the better of me. So I conceded. I had nothing to go on anyway, which wasn't just frustrating, it was frightening.

Bel was somewhere out there—alone...maybe cold...probably hungry. I couldn't bear the idea, but if I didn't let at least that much go, if I wallowed in what could be happening to him, if I gave even the smallest of horrors a chance to fester, I'd crumble.

Heading to the laundry room, I pulled my comfortable old sweater from a hook on the wall and drove my arms into it with a shiver as I buried my nose in the soft, worn threads. The brush of metal against the skin of my neck as I disturbed the amulet my father had given me last summer comforted me.

He'd said the necklace was a symbol he was always near, and right now I needed all the comfort I could get.

Rest. I would rest so I could be at my sharpest for Belfry.

Padding toward the parlor, I pushed my feet through pine tree limbs and shattered ornaments, clearing a path with Whiskey and Strike in tow. I looked away from the mess of my beautiful Christmas tree, the sticky puddle of coffee and caramel on the buffet table, and dropped down into my favorite chair by the fireplace hearth.

Reaching for the remote, I tapped in the digits for The Hallmark Channel with my thumb without even looking. That's just how acquainted I am with this channel—we're old friends. Bel and I had watched a hundred of their movies over the years while he mocked and teased my gooey sentimentality and I defended the need for a time out from the real world.

I'm a romantic at heart, and it doesn't have to have anything to do with me personally, I just love a happily-ever-after, especially if it involves Christmas.

Win and Arkady cut off my thoughts when they gasped in unison.

I sat up straight, tucking my sweater around me. "*What?*"

"Someone has stolen the kissy-face channel, too?" Arkady asked. "This is an act of terrorism! I will not let this blatant torture of my tangy blackberry jam stand!"

My eyes rose to meet the big-screen TV on the wall across from the fireplace to see what they were talking about, and I gasped, too.

My cable company's message sat at the bottom of the screen and read: You do not subscribe to this channel. Please call your cable provider for further information.

That son of a butt scratcher had cancelled my Hall-mark Channel subscription on top of everything else?

So not only had he likely kidnapped Belfry, and obliterated my Christmas decorations, but he'd yanked the final straw from my stack and taken the one thing that had any hope of easing my pain?

Aw, heck no. This would not stand. Someone had to pay.

"Argh!" I yelled my frustration at the dark screen, gripping the remote so hard I thought I might crack the plastic. "He cancelled The Hallmark Channel, boys. You know what this means, right?"

"Someone will lose fingers?" Arkady shouted out. "I can show you technique so good, no surgeon will ever be able to sew them back on!"

I blanched. I was into self-defense—all the way—but torture made my stomach hurt.

"Now, now, old friend. You must keep your compo-sure. We'll get online and reorder it and all will be right as rain, right, Stephania?"

"Right, but only after I cut off his fingers and reat-tach his thumbs to his nose!" I seethed, clenching my teeth.

Arkady gargled a laugh "Hah! There's my mini-spy! You will have your channel back in no time."

It wasn't enough to take everything else, he had to take this one last thing—that one last bit of Christmas I held a dear tradition.

My eyes narrowed. Someone had to pay —*would* pay.

After I rested of course. I wanted to be especially sharp when I broke out the cigar cutter—Arkady's personal favorite for chopping off fingers.

With the thought of sweet vengeance to warm me, I took a deep breath and let my grainy eyes slide shut.

~

The gentle pressure of someone's hand on my arm, warm and steady, woke me. "Stevie-girl? You got a turkey in your kitchen. Anything I should know?"

I stirred, my body one big ache. "It's a long story. Know anyone who wants a turkey they swear on their grandmother's soul they won't eat?"

He barked a familiar, comforting laugh. "Enzo's here now, and it's all gonna be okay. We'll figure out the turkey. Until then, I brought you some coffee. Wake up, gal. C'mon. It's freshly brewed, chockful of hazel-nut, chocolate and cinnamon, just the way you like. Made a special Christmas concoction just for you. If you wake up, I'll put a mountain of cream the size of Kilimanjaro on it, toooo," he sang near my ear in his light New York accent.

The seductive call of Enzo's coffee wafted beneath my nose, tendrils of rich, chocolatey steam filling up my nostrils. My eyes popped open and flew to my phone still in my lap, noting it was already seven a.m.

I bolted upright, that dread so deeply imbedded in

my stomach last night sitting in the pit of my belly like dead weight.

Belfry. Where are you?

I took the coffee with grateful hands and smiled up at a man who'd become quite dear to us. "Enzo, I'm so glad you're here. Thank you for the coffee."

He chucked me under the chin and smiled his broad smile, his wide face filling with Enzo's brand of gruff kindness. "You had a rough night, huh, kiddo? Saw the mess out there. I'll get the boys over today and we'll make it good as new. Don't you worry."

I motioned to the couch with a yawn. "You don't have to do that. Carmella's going to be home soon. You have other things to do, but please sit with me, Enzo. Tell me what happened yesterday? Did you see anything? Hear anything?"

He yanked his baseball cap off his head and scruffed a beefy hand over his short hair as he dropped down on the couch, pushing my Santa throw pillows to the other end.

His eyes fell to his hands as he worried his fingers over the brim of his cap. "I'll tell you exactly what I told the police. I had to leave a little early yesterday and everything was just fine. One of the boys in my crew got hurt on the job. Tried to text you, but it wouldn't go through. When I couldn't get in touch with you, I called Petula and told her I had to skedaddle. Said I'd leave the key for the guy comin' to set up. That was darn foolish of me, I suppose, but I figured we could trust Edmund. He's one of Petula's, after all. I'm sure sorry, gal."

"No, Enzo. Please don't blame yourself. It wasn't your fault at all. Both you and Carmella are so good to me. I couldn't ask for better friends."

"Sure feel like I let you down," he grumbled, tucking a thumb into his overalls.

"Never," I said on a grateful smile. "So you didn't see Edmund, but did you hear anything? Anything strange during the day while you were here working?"

"It's the darnedest thing, Stevie. I just can't believe…" He hitched a thumb over his shoulder toward the window facing the front lawn. "I don't understand how somebody could do so much damage in such a short amount of time. I didn't leave that early. It couldn'ta been more than maybe twenty minutes earlier than the original time I'd planned to leave."

Days like this—moments like this, where I wanted to spill my guts to the man who'd been such a constant in my life since I'd moved back to Eb Falls—came filled with guilt. He and Carmella treated me like one of their own, and I repaid them by deceiving them day in, day out.

Sometimes I had trouble coming to terms with that, and then I remembered hearing the explanation Win had given Arkady. Aloud, the idea I'm an ex-witch who had a couple of dead spies and a bat as her besties sounded absurd. How could I explain that to Carmella and Enzo and keep the conversation remotely rational?

Most of the people in town already thought I was

bananapants, as it stood with all the alleged talking to not just myself, but ghosts. Add in this enormous house I lived in alone with a dog and it would only make the truth appear so much kookier.

For now, I couldn't risk losing these people I'd come to care for, or put them in danger by telling them about my past. Thus, I remained silent.

"The police, Enzo… They questioned you?"

"Yep, they sure did," he said, his lips going thin. "Kept me in that little room where they try and get in your head by making you wait until they talk to ya. But they ain't gonna get old Enzo. I watch the cop shows. I know stuff."

I leaned forward and grabbed his hand, giving it a tight squeeze. "I'm glad you stayed strong. But you didn't really have anything to tell them anyway. So there's nothing to worry about."

"Yeah, but that one you call Starsky all the time? He always makes me feel like I did somethin' even when I'm as innocent as a newborn baby. He's what we used to call back in the old neighborhood…greasy. Yeah. Greasy. That's him."

I pressed Enzo's calloused knuckles to my cheek and inhaled the scent of sawdust and his aftershave before letting go. "Have the police heard anything else? Found anything else out since they left here?"

He leaned forward on the couch and looked me in the eye. "I only heard 'em mumblin' somethin' or other about the smarty-pants chef when I was on my way. They kept me in that room for almost four hours, waitin' around 'til they finally decided to talk to me, Stevie. I wasn't as sharp leavin' as I was goin' in. But I know what I heard," he grumbled before wrapping his fingers around his insulated cup and tipping it to his lips. "But I sure like the new gal, though. She's not as testy and jumpy as Starsky. Got a nice smile, too. She's a keeper."

My ears perked up, the tips growing hot. "What did you hear them say about Chef Le June, Enzo?"

"They found somethin' strange in his blood... No!" He paused, sticking a thick finger in the air. "They said they found something in his preliminary tox reports. Yeah. That was it!"

"Strange?"

"Yeah, the one who's always dressed like he's gettin' his picture taken for cop of the year was talking to the other one. Sandwich, I think it is. He said they found somethin' strange they couldn't identify in that Romeo's tox report."

Sipping at my coffee while trying to savor the special blend Enzo had created and forcing myself to focus on anything but Bel, I asked my next question carefully.

"You call Chef Le June 'Romeo'? Why's that?"

Enzo garbled a thick laugh filled with scorn in the back of his throat. "All us guys on the crew call him that, Stevie. He's always runnin' around town with someone new."

"Aha! The chef plays dirty pool!" Arkady shouted, almost making me jump. "I had bad feeling after we hear he has a wife while he dabbles with caterer Petula. Bad chef!"

Poor Petula... "Who's he running around town with, Enzo?"

Enzo's eyes went from lighthearted to dark and stormy as he squinted at me. "All sortsa girls. Saw him just the other day with that Cassie Haverstack."

I fought a gasp. "You mean the definition of soccer mom, Cassie Haverstack?" Her husband was an investment banker in Seattle. Well known, well respected. They had two children, a dog, and a beautiful house in one of Eb Falls' most exclusive gated communities.

"That's exactly who I mean. The one who wears all the yoga pants and her dog's sweater always matches hers. I know I shoulda told Petula I saw them off whisperin' real close in each other's ears at the dog park, but then I figured what I don't know as truth can't hurt Petula. Maybe all that whisperin' has to do with somethin' totally innocent. But they were mighty close under the cover of that mini-van door of hers. Maybe she was just orderin' up some cake for one of her PTA meetings? Least ways that's what I'd like to think."

I uncurled my legs from beneath me and sat forward. "But Chef Le June doesn't even have a dog. Why would he go to a dog park?"

Enzo began to rise, wiping his palms over his customary overalls. "That's what I was thinkin', but it ain't my business, kiddo. So I kept right on drivin' by."

"Have you heard about him hanging 'round anyone else?" I almost outwardly cringed asking the question, but I had to know if there were more suspects to consider. Every piece of information about Pascal, no matter how big or small, counted at this point.

Enzo rocked from foot to foot. "I've heard all sorts of stuff 'bout that guy, Stevie. But I can't report on any of it except what I saw with my own eyes. Don't wanna cause trouble with gossip, but I can sure tell ya, there's plenty of talk going around."

How did I miss this kind of stuff? Somehow I always managed to get wind of the gossip about *me*.

Rising, I set my coffee down and gave Enzo a hug, which he returned by enveloping me in his bear-like embrace. "I'm sorry you got in the middle of all this, Enzo. I don't know what's going on or why Pascal was even here, but I hate that you were involved."

Giving me one last squeeze, he scrubbed his knuckles over the top of my head in his typical affectionate gesture and set me from him. "Don't you worry about none of that. Now, we're still having Christmas dinner together, right? Your family, my family, that father of yours who can't stop looking in the mirror?"

I laughed and nodded, my heart clenching at the mention of my father. "Yes. *The* Hugh Granite will be here, along with my mother, Dita."

Dita and I had come a long way since the summer. A long way. I'd venture to say we were bonding in a very light, occasional-mani/pedi, ladies-who-lunch way.

And Hugh? Hugh was always texting me, calling me from Japan, sending me DVDs of his old and newest movie releases. He'd captured me in his crazy ego-driven web in the best way possible. I found I could actually count on him, and that warmed me from the inside out. He was the father I'd so craved as a kid times a million.

I knew he was making up for not being around when I was a child. He didn't admit as much, and truly, it was hardly his fault. My mother never told him about me, but he'd made being my father his mission.

Enzo gave me a hearty pat on the back. "Good. He makes me laugh, but mostly, I like how happy you get when he's around. Now don't forget, Carmella's gonna be here early to cook with you."

"How could I forget she's going to teach me the secret to keeping my turkey moist, and how to make her sage, apple, and sausage stuffing from scratch? I wouldn't miss it for the world, Enzo."

Chucking me under the chin, he grinned, the lines on his forehead meeting his raised eyebrows. "Lookin' forward to it. Gonna go call some of the guys to help clean up out there and figure out your turkey. Won't take long with the whole crew. So don't give me any guff, gal."

I blew him a kiss as he raised his wide hand in retreat and stomped out into the entryway. The closing of the door meant I could finally stop pretending everything was all right.

"No word from Bel, I take it, Dove?"

My chest went tight and my anxiety shot to a new

level. "None since last night. But I think you know what we have to do, don't you?"

Both Win and Arkady groaned in longwinded unison, neither of them lovers of Cassie and her group of soccer moms. "Talk to Cassie Haverstock?"

Heading toward the stairs, coffee in hand, I just needed to brush my teeth and we were good to go. "Yes. As far as I'm concerned, she's now a suspect. I know you're not fans of the yoga ladies, boys, but it has to be done. Who knows if Chef Bed Hopper was seeing more than just Cassie and Petula? Cassie might have names, and the names of more women could lead to an explanation for why he was here last night instead of Edmund. So maybe, at least until we hear something from Bel again, we can piece his disappearance together via Chef Le June's half of the story. Let's just hope the police don't get to her before we do or she might clam up on us."

"But weren't you the one who said we didn't even know if this was a murder investigation?" Win reminded me in his cocky British way.

"I was. But now there are tox reports with quote-unquote strange things showing up. I want to know what those strange things are, and while I think about how I'm going to find out, talking to Cassie will keep my mind busy and make me feel like I'm doing something."

"So can we officially call this a murder investigation, Mini-Spy?"

"Only if you promise to wipe the drool from your chin when you do."

Win's laughter followed me up the stairs and well into my bedroom, where I caught sight of Bel's favorite nesting plant. The elephant ear plant where he curled up every day in order to nap.

As I brushed my teeth and sent out another mental call to Belfry, only to be greeted with complete silence, I finally allowed myself the luxury of a good, hard cry.

CHAPTER 8

"*A*ren't you that Madam Spooky who has the shop over on Main?" Cassie Haverstock asked me as she rewrapped her trendy scarf around her neck on her way out the door of Joy Carmichael's yoga studio.

She'd been easy enough to find—most of the wealthier moms in Eb Falls attended yoga. They took the early classes after dropping their children at school —which left plenty of time during their days to take the dog to the park and maybe—just maybe—have an affair with a sexy chef.

I held my hand out and smiled. I'd had the where-withal to at least put on one of my better thrift store cashmere sweater finds in a soft crimson, coupling it with my own trendy gray-and-purple scarf, jeans, and black knee-high boots.

Okay, so my hair was a little off its game, but I didn't have time to fluff and poof, and my eyeliner was probably drifting toward my cheeks. But all in all, I didn't look homeless.

"Yeah. That's me. Madam Spooky, or as my customers call me, Madam Zoltar. Well, that's my stage name, if you will. My real name's Stevie Cartwright. I live over in the big house on Samantha Lane..." I purposely let her know I owned Mayhem Manor so she'd realize we were on equal financial footing here.

I'd heard about this woman and how dismissive she could be if you weren't of her financial ilk, and today wasn't a day Cassie Haverstock wanted to test how much I despised that sort of mentality.

But Cassie surprised me by giving me a warm if not practiced smile. It didn't quite reach her hazel eyes, wide with surprise and fringed with eyelash extensions, but it did say, "I bet I have a charity you can donate wads of cash to, Stevie Cartwright."

"Wow. The séance business has been good to you, huh? It's so nice to meet you! I'm sorry I haven't gotten around to it sooner. We love our local businesses. We'd love to have you come to one of our events, Stevie."

With my checkbook, of course. "That would be lovely. I'm always happy to donate to a good cause. Until then, do you mind if I ask you a couple of questions? I'd be happy to buy you a coffee for a minute of your time."

I pointed over my shoulder toward Forrest's shop, Strange Brew, and smiled as much as my face would allow with the sharp breeze making my lips stick to my teeth.

"As long as you don't mind the mess I'm in. I mean, look at me, would you? And I drink tea. Chai tea, actually. Caffeine increases your blood pressure."

"Right. So tea then?" I asked as I began to walk before the hoard of women piled out of the yoga studio and we found ourselves caught up in the clouds of expensive perfume and perspiration, with plenty of curious stares.

Cassie followed along beside me, smoothing a hand over the headband that kept her raven ponytail away from her angular face. In the gloomy, overcast day, her pale skin appeared almost gray, making the slash of red lipstick on her mouth rather garish.

Still, she was beautiful, and maintained from head to toe to within an inch of her life—even after a sweaty yoga class.

Pulling the door open to Strange Brew to the tune of the cheerful Christmas bells jingling on the handle, I waved to Forrest, who was behind the counter, and winked at Chester, who peered over his morning paper with one bushy eyebrow cocked in question.

I pulled one of the ice-cream-colored chairs out with a smile and motioned for Cassie to sit. Naturally, she looked calm and collected amidst Forrest's busy cafe, a beautiful, pastel-colored background for a woman who appeared to have it all.

Sliding gracefully into the chair opposite me, Cassie crossed her toned, slender legs, folded her hands and waited.

Awkward silence ensued between us as customers

bustled in and out and the jazzy tunes of Kenny G playing "Jingle Bells" wafted through the speakers.

Cassie and I had little to nothing in common but big bank accounts, so polite small talk was pointless. After one of the waitresses took our orders, I decided full steam ahead was the only way to approach this.

I watched her from beyond the brim of my cup with careful eyes, unsure how to proceed until I decided I was looking for the one steady in my life—the one constant, reliable source of love and support I'd ever had. It was all or nothing in honor of Bel.

"Look, Cassie, I'm just going to be blunt here. I think we both know we don't have a lot in common. Being in different places in our lives and all."

Her eyes narrowed ever so slightly as she, too, sipped her tea, her eyes darting about the festively decorated room before finally settling on me. "You mean you being single and living all alone in that big house on the Sound, and me being happily married with children?"

I had to admire her guns-a-blazin' leap into our conversation. It was refreshing. "That's exactly what I mean. But we do have one thing in common."

Her plucked raven eyebrow rose. "Money?"

"Chef Le June."

Her eyebrow lost its jaunty position and her face went paler than the norm. "What about him?" she asked in a clipped tone, almost too quickly for my comfort.

"He's dead. You did hear, didn't you? He died at my house last night."

Looking over her shoulder, she let her chin rest on the cap of it when she shrugged with a hint of indifference. "I heard it was probably a heart attack. Poor Petula."

"And poor you?"

Cassie's sharp intake of breath indicated she knew she'd been caught. Twisting her scarf around her neck, she eyed me without even trying to hide her venom. "Meaning?"

I wasn't going to play cat and mouse with this woman. I had no personal grudge against her, but Belfry missing canceled out decorum.

"Meaning you've been seen with Chef Le June in close quarters. If I tell the police I heard information about a certain meeting in a dog park, they're sure to want to question you. That could be awkward for you and your happy marriage, couldn't it?"

"Subtle, Dove. Very smooth indeed," Win remarked in a dry tone.

"Bah with your subtle, Winterbutt. Go for her throat, my jelly donut! Squeeze until she cries cousin!"

I fought a smile and waited for Cassie to answer, keeping my expression as passive as possible.

"Are you telling me you won't tell the police you saw me with him if I tell you what was going on?"

I had two choices here. One, I could use this to get what I wanted, which could amount to nothing more than her telling me they were playing footsie. But there was the small chance Cassie knew he'd been playing footsies with other women, too, just as Enzo had implied.

She might even know the names of those other women, and they could possibly provide an answer as to why chef was at my house instead of Edmund in the first place. But more, if he had in fact been murdered, they could be potential suspects.

Or I could simply be honest and tell her Enzo had likely already confessed what he'd seen to the police last night and that's how I knew about the affair. Clearly, the police hadn't questioned her yet, but I suspected they wouldn't be far behind me.

I decided to fib—because not even my integrity was going to keep me from finding Belfry. "That's exactly what I'm saying. Were you having an affair with Pascal?"

"Fine," she huffed with a roll of her eyes. "But it wasn't exactly an affair. We didn't love each other or anything so sappy. It was more like an agreement. Pascal was a man with...a large, varied appetite, is probably how I'd label it. I called, he came—until he showed up one day smelling like some French tart. I can abide plenty, but to literally hop from one mistress to another within what could have been only minutes is uncouth at best. So I ended it. No fuss, no muss. Do you understand?"

Oui, oui. I totally understood that kind of arrangement. "So I assume this varied and large appetite was appeased by a buffet of women? More than just the perfumed French tart?"

Cassie's mouth thinned and her posture stiffened. I had to imagine hearing that out loud was a hit to her ego—even if their arrangement was very modern. "I'm sure there was."

"And that didn't bother you?"

"Should it? Listen, Miss Cartwright. I have a family. A husband. A home. Pascal was just a fun distraction. If he was playing in other sandboxes, he kept it to himself. I only know there was gossip about it but no names were ever mentioned."

I fought with everything I had to keep my objectivity for the sake of finding Belfry, but it wasn't easy. After my ex-fiancé left me at the altar, I wasn't a fan of infidelity for obvious reasons, but Cassie had children. Distractions hurt children. No one knew that better than me.

"You said there was gossip about Pascal playing in other sandboxes. Who did you hear talk about these other women?"

Now she fidgeted, fingering a petal on the fake white poinsettia in the vase on the table. "I honestly can't remember, and that's absolutely all I have to say. I've owned my part in this. You won't get anything else out of me because I don't know anything else."

Bet if I put her in my super-duper spy hold she'd remember. Still, something in my gut told me it wasn't worth it to force the information out of her.

Pulling my gloves from my purse as an indication

our conversation was over, I asked one last question for no other reason than to have the answer.

"Where were you last night, Cassie?"

"Getting ready for the Christmas Lights Display Contest that never was. Though, I hear *you* had quite a display."

Win said disarming your opponent by doing something they didn't see coming often caught them off guard. So I ignored her barb by smiling at her. "Do you have any witnesses to confirm your alibi?"

She scoffed at me, leaning back in her chair and crossing her arms over her chest in a defensive pose. "An alibi? What are you, a part-time police officer, too? You really are the busy bee, aren't you?"

Now, if all of Win's lessons panned out, it was time for me to take control by reminding Cassie who was in charge. "No, but I suppose we could always take a spin down to the police station and put in my application."

Cassie's lips pursed, but her eyes appeared resigned. "You can ask Merrill Mathers or Taryn Johnson. We were all outside making last-minute contest preparations before the judges' arrival."

Pulling my gloves on, I tightened the scarf around my neck. "May I ask just one more thing before I let you go?"

Her eyes flashed fire at me, her anger obvious, but she shrugged dismissively. "Do I have a choice? You did just blackmail me."

Instantly, I became irritated. She was a married

woman with a dead afternoon delight and she was calling me a blackmailer? The nerve.

I couldn't tell her the real reason I was desperate for even a tiny bit of information that might lead to Bel, but I wasn't going to allow her to turn me into the bad guy either.

"Oh, please, Cassie. Don't play the victim. You're hardly innocent. You were cheating on your husband, after all."

That really burnt my britches. Yes, I know it's because my mother has a jaded past full of other women's husbands, but even if she didn't, I still wouldn't agree with infidelity.

"Then get on with it and be done. I have somewhere to be," she snapped, rolling her hand in a gesture of impatience.

My fists clenched around the handle of my purse, but I managed to keep my temper in check. "Did Petula know about the other women Pascal was fooling around with? Did she know about you?"

"Nope. As far as I know, she was blind as the proverbial bat. Whether that was intentional or not, I don't know. I turned a blind eye to it, so I can't throw stones," she said, her tone icy as she scooped up her tea. "Are we done here now?"

Sucking in my cheeks, I rose and picked up my coffee. "I think we are. Have a lovely, infidelity-free day, Cassie."

"Bazinga!" Arkady shouted in my ear, quoting Sheldon from *Big Bang Theory*, one of his favorite shows. But it only made me feel guilty for the inability to keep my personal feelings out of my investigation.

Turning my back to Cassie, I made my way to the counter, where Forrest was busy arranging muffins in the front counter case.

His head popped up, his chestnut-colored hair shiny under the recessed lighting above us. "Hello, pretty lady! Can I interest you in a muffin?" Forrest wiggled his eyebrows and held my favorite apple/blueberry muffin with crumbs on top in the palm of his hand, but my appetite was nil at this point.

"No, but thanks, Forrest. You're very sweet."

"Hey, can I talk to you for a minute?" He hitched his sharp jaw toward the back in the area of the kitchen.

"Is it important? I really have to run." *And find my missing familiar.*

"You always have to run, Stevie."

Uh-oh. I knew that tone. That was the tone Forrest used when he was getting frustrated with my busy schedule and jam-packed life. Granted, I hadn't seen a lot of him lately, especially with the Christmas Lights Display Contest taking up so much of my time.

Though we didn't really have any kind of dating understanding, there'd been a time or two when he'd expressed his wish to see more of me. But I guess the question really was, did I want to see more of Forrest?

Why wouldn't I want to see more of Forrest?

I think I've said as much before, I like him a lot. He's attractive and hardworking and smart, but... It was the "but" in the equation; I continually struggled to find the words to fill in the blank.

If nothing else, I wanted to keep things easy between us. I didn't want hard feelings, but I didn't want to lead Forrest on either, and lately he'd been hinting at something more. And while he hinted, I ran in the other direction because...

Because?

Following him to the kitchen, I pushed the swinging doors open and poked my head around the corner. "I'm sorry, Forrest. Please don't be upset. It's just been a crazy time with this Chef Le June business and whatever happened to my house last night. What's up?"

He rolled his tongue along the inside of his cheek when he glanced at me. I assumed he was trying to decide whether he wanted to ask me something, but then his shoulders relaxed and he smiled his handsome smile.

"I was hoping you might have some free time tonight. Maybe we could grab dinner before the holiday rush? I'd like to talk to you about something."

My shoulders sagged in defeat. Any other night and I'd have gladly gone. "I..."

"Can't, right?" he asked on a sigh full of resignation as he pulled off his apron and dropped it on the shiny island, where the makings of more delicious muffins sat by an industrial blender.

Regret stabbed me hard, yet what could I say? I

can't have dinner with you because I think my familiar's been kidnapped? "I'm sorry, Forrest—"

But he held up his hand and shook his head as he approached me. "It's fine, Stevie." Then he paused and gripped my shoulders, looking down at me with serious eyes. "Listen, can I ask you something? And I want you to be really honest with me. Let's just get everything out in the open."

I hesitated for a moment, my stomach churning. I think I knew what he was going to ask me, I just wasn't sure how to answer. "Of course. You can ask me anything."

"Is it someone else you're waiting around for? Someone you hope to get back together with? Someone you can't forget?"

I'm sure my eyes revealed my confusion and my evasion. What was it holding me back from dating him full time? Forrest was everything any sane woman could want. *But...* There was that word again.

For lack of anything better to say, I stuttered, "I don't know what you mean."

"You *do* know what I mean, Stevie. Why can't you fully commit to dating me? Is it someone else?"

"But that's crazy, Forrest. Who else could there be? If I were dating someone else, don't you think you'd know about it? I mean, nothing is much of a secret here in Eb Falls."

His hands fell away from my shoulders and he took a step back, his body language saying tense with a side of frustrated. "I dunno. Maybe it's someone from your past? A bad relationship you can't get over? I have no idea. I just know you duck and run a lot, and while I dislike ultimatums, I find myself thinking about throwing one at you more than I care to admit."

My throat grew tight and threatened to choke off my next words, but I managed to get them out. "I like you, Forrest. I like you so much. I'm just not ready…"

"Ready to find out if we could be something more." His nod was sharp as he appeared to accept his words —which weren't far off the mark, by the way. "Well, I *am* ready. I guess we're just in two different places, and that's okay. But in the meantime, I won't be a place card for someone else while you figure it out."

I'd never looked at it like that. I'd never meant for it to be like that. Reaching for his arm, I gripped it, only managing to grab onto the sleeve of his shirt. "I…I…"

He took another step backward and shook his head once more, loosening my hand from his sleeve as he did. "It's okay, Stevie. Really. I get it. I just needed to hear it straight for a change."

Tears began to fill my eyes. I didn't want this between us—us at odds like this, awkward and weird— but it was unfair of me to hope we could occasionally see one another if Forrest was looking for someone steady.

I was prepared to say as much when I heard Petula's hysteria-filled voice from the dining area. "How could you, Cassie Haverstock! How could you do something like this to me?"

CHAPTER 9

y eyes met Forrest's just before I flew back out to the dining area to find Petula, her face jammed into Cassie Haverstock's as she used her body to keep her cornered right next to the tabletop Christmas tree Chester and I had decorated only a couple of weeks ago.

The ornaments bounced on the limbs of the small tree as Petula widened her threatening stance, cramping Cassie until she had no means of escape.

"Petula!" I yelled as I ran to the far corner and gripped her shoulders to pull her from Cassie. "Stop, Petula!"

When she whirled around, losing her focus on Cassie, Petula looked like she'd been through the wringer. Her hair stuck out at awkward angles from her head, strands stuck together as though she'd aimed wrong with her hair gel. Her soft eyes were wild as she finally appeared to truly see me. The moment she looked up at me, she crumpled, her typically smiling face falling way to complete misery.

"Did you hear, Stevie?" she cried.

I couldn't bear her humiliation on front of everyone in the café. "Come with me, Petula. Come sit with me and tell me what's going on," I coaxed, in an attempt to get her away from Cassie, who was simply green about her paler-than-pale gills.

As though she now realized she'd made a scene, Petula slumped against me, trembling.

"How dare you attack me in a public place, you animal!" Cassie accused, sticking a finger in the air in Petula's direction, her voice pitched high and full of outrage.

But her outrage didn't last long when I glared at her as Chester physically took Petula from me and led her to a table.

I leaned into Cassie "Downward Facing Dog Queen" Haverstock and whispered with deliberate menace, "I'm pretty sure you have somewhere else to be, don't you? I'm also pretty sure you don't want me to share where you've *been*, now do you?"

"Ah. Intimidation looks good on you, my petal!"

"Go home, Cassie. To you *husband and children*," I hissed before hitching my thumb toward the door.

While everyone in the café sat stock-still in shock in their chairs, Cassie narrowed her eyes at me and lifted her haughty chin before she stomped off, no longer the graceful gazelle she'd been when we'd first sat down.

Satisfied she was gone, I rushed to Petula, who'd

crumpled in a chair next to Chester. He eyed her with concern, his warm gaze riddled with sympathy. "Ya okay there, Petula? Lemme get you some coffee and we'll fix this right up. Got peppermint sticks, too. That'll make it better." He patted her hand and went off in search of peppermint sticks.

That's when she began to cry in earnest, tears pouring down her face and dropping on the table in salty splashes.

"Tell me what happened, Petula. Please. What's going on?"

Of course, I already knew what was going on. Somehow, I guess Petula had gotten wind of the fact that Cassie Haverstock was messing around with Pascal. Gosh, I don't know if I could have felt any worse for Petula. She'd been so crazy about the chef and he was nothing more than a full-on rake.

"She's been lying to me, Stevie! Lying to me all this time. All while I helped her plan her big New Year's Eve party—all this time!" she whimpered, gasping for air.

"Oh, Petula, I'm sorry. Tell me what I can do to make this better," I asked, stroking her arm.

"You can go give that Taryn Johnson a piece of your mind, that's what! All this time Cassie knew Pascal was playing around with that woman and she never said a word! I thought we were friends. How could she let me look like such a fool?"

Taryn Johnson?

"Taryn Johnson?" Win's words mirrored my

thoughts. "Bloody hell, Stevie. He was a jolly old cad, wasn't he? Poor sweet Petula."

"Pascal was fooling around with Taryn Johnson?"

"That dirty bird!" she fairly shouted on a renewed breath of air. "And Cassie knew! I *know* she knew because the police talked to two witnesses who told them so!"

Chester came back with the coffee and promised peppermint stick, setting them in front of Petula with a squeeze to her shoulder. Her hands shook as she gathered the cup in her chubby hands and held it close to her chest.

"Who told the police about Taryn, Petula?" And why hadn't she heard Cassie had also been doing the do with Pascal?

"Merrill Mathers, that's who! Everyone's talking about it and laughing at me behind my back."

Oh, boy. Pascal had made his way around the cul-de-sac and back again, hadn't he? I'd bet my eyeteeth Merrill wasn't entirely innocent in this either.

"Now, now, P. That ain't true. If anything, they're all thinking what a fool he was to mess around with a married woman when he had a good woman like you," Chester soothed.

But Petula wasn't hearing anyone or anything at this point. She set the coffee away from her, the liquid sloshing out of the cup and onto the table. She'd very clearly realized everyone was trying not to stare as she pushed back her chair, keeping her voice low.

"I have to go. I have to go *now*! I just came to get

some coffee for everyone because we're all so tired. I—I didn't expect to see that woman is all. She caught me off guard, but I can't stay. We still can't find Edmund and we all need some coffee to keep us going so we can continue to search for him."

I hopped out of my chair along with Petula. "You still haven't found Edmund?" My concern ratcheted up ten notches.

Pushing her mussed hair from her eyes, she tightened her sweater around her waist and shook her head. "No. No one can find him anywhere. He never made it to the mayor's house, and we still don't know why Pascal was at your house instead of him. When Edmund left the shop, he said he was going to your house. That's the last anyone saw or heard from him, Stevie. I told you that last night."

The worry in Petula's voice matched my internal anxiety. Where was Edmund? But I didn't press the issue because just as I was preparing to help Petula get back to her shop, one of her employees breezed in the door, her eyes full of concern when she directed her gaze at Petula.

"Oh, thank goodness you're all right, Petula!" Elise Timmons called out. "We were getting worried. C'mon. Let's get those coffees and get you back to the shop. You need to rest," she chastised, wrapping her arm around Petula and guiding her toward the counter.

I wanted to ask Petula a million questions about Edmund and the gorgeous pastry Pascal allegedly left for me, but her being so frazzled, on top of publicly humiliated, made me decide to wait.

"What a dog," Chester said with disgust, his eyes full of anger. "Feel bad for the old girl. She's a good woman, and he hoodwinked her six ways to Sunday."

I nodded my sympathy and sighed. "Me, too. He hoodwinked me for sure. I had no idea Pascal was so—er, busy. He has a wife, too, you know, and a bunch of women he's been fooling around with, and I never even suspected."

Chester winked and grinned, driving a thumb under his red and white Christmas-themed suspenders. "That's because you're too busy talking to dead people."

I forced a smile before dropping a kiss on top of Chester's balding head. "I have to go, Chester. But I'll see you for the Christmas Eve party at church, right?"

"You betcha." As I turned to leave, he grabbed my hand, his warm fingers enveloping mine. "Hey, can I ask ya somethin'?"

I cocked my head in question due to his tone, so solemn and serious. "Anytime."

"We can still be friends even if you and the kid don't work out, can't we?"

My heart tightened in my chest and those tears I'd been fighting all day long threatened to fall. "Always, Chester. That's a promise," I whispered, making my escape from Strange Brew before I openly sobbed.

As I gulped in the fresh air of the chilly day, I beeped my car and opened the door.

"Are you all right, Dove?"

Sighing, I slid inside and turned the heat up, pressing my forehead to the steering wheel. "Jolly good."

"I'm sorry about Forrest."

"You heard?"

"No, no. I would never eavesdrop on something so private. That is our agreement and always will be. But Chester's question tipped me off."

I couldn't talk to Win about Forrest. Not because he wouldn't listen, even if Forrest wasn't his favorite person, but because it felt like I should keep my feelings about him to myself.

"How about we review what we've learned so far and where to go from here?" I asked, changing the subject. "Arkady, you in?"

"*Dah, malutka*. I am always in. Should we go talk to the naughty cul-de-sac women next? This Merrill who spilled her jellybeans at the police station?"

Biting my cheek, I shook my head. "I don't know. Okay, so Merrill threw her friend under the bus. Lots of people apparently had affairs with Chef Le June. Cassie made it sound as though breaking it off with him after smelling, and I quote, 'a French tart's perfume,' was about as painful as having a hangnail. She didn't appear at all emotional about it. Did you get the sense she was broken up over Pascal fooling around?"

"Only that he had the audacity to do so mere

moments before he was with her. I'd say it was more ego than heartbreak," Win answered.

Arkady mock-shivered in my ear. "Brrr. She is cold like fish in icy pond in Krakow."

"That's how I felt, too. Cassie certainly didn't scream murderer. Though, not wanting her husband to find out about the affair would surely give her motive to kill him. But then if Pascal were fooling around with a bunch of women, he wouldn't want their husbands to know either. It isn't like he'd tell anyone. So what about Taryn? Is she the jealous type? Maybe, unlike Cassie, she was angry she wasn't the only woman Pascal was seeing?"

"Maybe," Win drawled. "And what about the husbands themselves? They're certainly large enough to drag Pascal outside. A jealous husband is an unpredictable beast. Have they all been accounted for?"

I poked a finger in the air. "Good point. I don't know why I didn't think of that." I actually *did* know why I didn't think of it. Because I wasn't thinking clearly. I was too close to this case, or whatever we were calling it. "I'll poke around and see what I can see.

"And that still leaves Edmund. There's foul play there for sure, but by bloody whom? Edmund was the most unassuming, gentle young man in the history of gentle young men. So why? Why would someone harm him? Unless he knew something he shouldn't."

Win's words made my chest tighten uncomfortably. But then dread filled my stomach when I had a terrible thought. "Maybe Edmund caught the person who messed with our decorations and they wanted to shut him up? Oh, Win. That would be awful. If magic really is involved... Poor Edmund."

"But then that still doesn't explain Chef Le June showing up. And if it was magic, no one had to physically change the decorations, Dove. Isn't it just a snap of some fingers? The wave of a wand?"

Running my fingers over my temples, I squeezed. "You'd think so. I mean, it's certainly easier to cast a spell than do all that manual labor. Believe me, if I still had my powers, I might have considered cheating a little. Hauling Santa up to the roof was more work than spy training ever was. And then there's the note allegedly left for me by the chef. That's a complete sham. We all know Pascal was too self-absorbed to care whether I relaxed or not. He'd never leave a note like that. I should have asked Petula if she knew anything about the opera cake, but she was so upset and frazzled... I think our next move is we go back and ask about the cake. I'm willing to lay bets that's what killed our chef. Maybe one of the women made it and poisoned him? Maybe the pastry had nothing to do with Adam or me at all?"

"So you think one of those spandex-clad, long-limbed, empathy-less gazelles could actually make an opera cake, Stevie? Bah," my Spy Guy groused.

Win had a point.

"Did you see the delicate layers of pastry? Witness how perfectly cut and aligned they were? How beautiful that single confection's shape was? Those women wouldn't spend that much time on a pastry they'd never eat unless it were infused with kale and the elusive tears of a Dutch maiden, Stevie. Imagine how much time they'd miss shopping and applying their makeup. No. I'm sorry. I don't buy the theory those women had anything to do with Chef Foo-Foo's murder. They're as self-absorbed as he was."

"This is dilemma, my friends. We have too many questions, not enough answers. We must see police and ask questions. Does big officer with stiff lips still owe you favor?"

"You mean Officer Nelson? The one with the stiff upper lip?" I shrugged, watching the rain batter the windshield. "I don't like to look at it as owing me anything, Arkady. I know that's not how you guys do things, and I'll admit, some of your tactics really work, as in the case of Cassie. But Dana's sort of my friend, too. I don't want to take advantage of him."

"That's because your heart is good like gold," Arkady said with a chuckle.

A sharp rap of knuckles on my window startled me, making me sit up straight to find Sandwich eyeing me as rain dripped from his plastic raincoat.

I pressed the button and rolled down the window to find him in a rather sour mood. "Talking to yourself again, Stevie?"

"Nope. Just the dead people," I joked.

But Sandwich didn't respond to my teasing. "You're in a loading zone, Stevie. If I've told you once, I've told you a thousand times, you can't park here."

Oh dear. Someone was awfully terse today. "Has it been a thousand?" I teased. "I thought last count was only like eight hundred and twelve."

"Move it or I'm going to ticket you, Stevie," he said from tightly compressed teeth.

"Sardine's having a bad day. Look out, Dove."

My eyes flew open wide in surprise. "Why so cranky?"

He planted his palms on the roof of my car and scowled down at me. "I'm not cranky. I'm just trying to do my job, and I can't do that if you're always giving me guff."

I smiled with sympathy. "Long night?"

"Very. Now are you gonna move or am I gonna have to call Jim and have you towed?"

"Jim Levine's towing now? I thought it was Benny June?" I looked up at him thoughtfully, waiting for an answer.

"Nope. Benny moved to Tampa to be closer to his daughter. Jim's our official guy now."

"Bet he was happy to see Benny leave. He rooted out the competition and he didn't even have to try, huh?"

Sandwich nodded his plastic-covered head, water from the rain spraying me in the face. "He wasn't sad, that's all I'll say. Now move along, please."

"When did this become a loading zone, anyway? I feel like you guys are always changing the rules on me when I'm not looking just to keep me out of your way."

"Stevie, stop arguing with me and get a move on

already. It's not enough I got the boss breathing down my neck about that chef's murder, but you gotta hassle me, too? Give a guy a break!"

And there it was. The official label.

Murder.

CHAPTER 10

"Murder? Chef Le June was murdered?"

"I called it!" Win cheered.

Sandwich's chin dropped to his chest as he let out a ragged sigh of defeat. "Dang it, Stevie, stop tripping me up all the time! You're always distracting me with your questions and your fancy interrogation tactics."

"Oh, baloney. If asking about Jim is interrogating you, there's much you need to learn about the art of interrogation, Grasshopper," I teased.

But Sandwich wasn't in a jokey mood. His lips clamped shut, making an angry line across his usually cheerful face. "You know what I mean, Stevie. You get to talkin', and I forget I'm an officer of the law and you're a nosy civilian and it's just like we're friends back in high school, jabberjawin' about gym class. Now leave it alone. That information's confidential."

Leaning into the window, I ignored the splashes of

rainwater and smiled up at Sandwich, trying to keep my tone carefree. "How was he murdered?"

"Aw, heck no, Cartwright. You're not gettin' anything else outta me. Didn't I just say it was confidential?"

I gave him a nonchalant shrug even though my stomach was turning itself inside out. "Well, yeah, but it's always confidential, Sandwich. Yet somehow I manage to find out anyway. So you might as well tell me how he was murdered and save us all the aggravation of Stevie Cartwright poking her nose in where it doesn't belong with her fancy interrogation tactics."

"I'm not telling you anything," he reaffirmed before slapping the roof of my car and backing up. "Now move it or lose it, Cartwright!" He bellowed the order, sputtering rainwater everywhere.

I rolled up the window with a huff and a frown and put my car in drive, pulling out of the space and moving up two to park in front of The Spice Shop so I could think in peace. We were on a fast train to nowhere here. Nothing was coming together.

"Steeviiee!"

I froze. Belfry!

My eyes instantly scanned the horizon for his tiny portly body, half expecting him to piston from the sky and land on my windshield. "Bel? Bel! Where are you?"

"Dove? You can hear him again?" The alarm in Win's voice served only to heighten my anxiety.

Both relief and terror rushed through me in a wave

as I peered into the cloudy, rain-swollen sky. "Yes! Do you see him? I can't see anything!"

"Stevie! It's...cold! Help us!" Bel's cries for help were choppy, full of static and broken. But then he called out again, *"Steeeeviieee! Help Us!"*

I sat back in the driver's seat and fought for breath. "Help us? *Us?*"

"Precious dumpling, what is happening? Talk to Arkady!"

Adrenaline sped the crash of my heart, leaving me shaky. "Bel said 'us'. He said 'help us'!" Tears filled my eyes again. "Who is *us*, Bel? Tell me where you are!"

There was more static and then he blurted out, *"Cake, Stevie! Don't ... the cake!"*

"Argh!" I screamed my frustration into the interior of the car. "The cake? What does that mean, Bel?" I listened again, listened so hard I thought my ears would fall off for the listening, but he was gone once more, leaving me with the image of him shaking and cold—an image I almost couldn't bear.

"Stephania! What's happening?" Win persisted, his tone jostling me from my worries.

"I don't know. He keeps fading in and out—like a static-filled radio, you know? He said 'help us' and 'don't the cake'. What does this all mean? Where could he be if he can still contact me?"

"While you sleep like small baby last night, I look all over these planes with Zero, *malutka*. He is not here. He must still be somewhere on your plane. That's good, yes?"

145

Do not cry. Do not cry. Do not cry, Stevie Cartwright. All hope's not lost if you can still hear him. I gritted my teeth together to keep from turning into a puddle of tears, more determined than ever to find Belfry.

"I think so. I mean, I don't know, Arkady. Who would take Bel? If it's you-know-who, using his magic, how are we going to fight something we can't see or who refuses to appear?"

I know my panic came through loud and clear in my tone, but the more I tried to beat it into submission, the deeper it burrowed inside me.

"Cake…" Win murmured, and I could hear he was working something out in his head. "Maybe he meant don't eat the cake? The pastries Chef Le June brought? As in, *you* shouldn't eat the cake? Maybe it truly is as you suspected, and the crumbs around his mouth were from his own pastries, and that's what killed him? I don't understand the connection between the two, but surely we need to question Petula, Stevie. I know you don't want to upset her any further, but we must speak to her. We can't afford to be delicate with Bel at stake."

I nodded my head, scraping a thumb under my eyes to wipe away my tears. *Get it together, Cartwright.*

"Agreed. While I do that, maybe you two can figure out what Bel meant by us. Come up with some theories, I don't know. Something. Anything. *Please.*"

"Us…" Win repeated.

Grabbing the door handle, I inhaled deeply but my hands shook. "Yes. He said help *us.* I don't know what that means, but he said it twice. It means something."

Win's aura wrapped around me, rocking me as Arkady reassured me with his typical tough guy approach. "We shall seek and destroy, kitten. I will break the fingers of every spirit I come into contact with until they tell me about this bad man who means you harm. We will find him. Now you go. Talk to Petula and ask about Chef Cheater's letter, *dah?*"

Shaking off my anxieties, I only nodded, pushing the door open and making a break for her shop through the pouring rain. Bursting through the door, I forced myself to slow down so I wouldn't make Petula any more anxious than she already was.

I loved Petula's shop, filled with samples for wedding cakes and gorgeous flower arrangements in pastel colors. She'd decorated the shop in silver and a pale green for Christmas, with pearlescent white accents, every spray of greenery on her counters and above the doorways dipped in a sugar-frosted white.

It almost always soothed me to wander through the vignettes Petula created with such ease. My eyes never missed the chance to roam over the rustic armoires and buffet tables she'd nestled into corners to display the various stemware and plates she offered to her clients.

But today all I could think about was her unwitting connection to Bel and that dirty cheat Chef Le June. It didn't help that the store was in total chaos, Petula's staff moving about frantically as some held cell phones to their ears and paced while others organized flyers with Edmund's picture on them.

They'd set up a search-party table for Edmund, and I was pleased to see the majority of her staff bustling about, each with a task. Under any other circumstance, I'd be out there beating the forest floor with my stick, helping the search party look for him as if he were my own. Edmund was a good kid, polite and sweet, and he deserved to have these people devote so much effort to recovering him.

But I was the only search party Bel had, and I couldn't tell anyone else about his disappearance. So while I hated insinuating myself into the middle of their efforts, I had little choice.

I spotted Petula by the kitchen door, still harried, her agitation clear as she glanced at a clipboard, holding it with trembling fingers. Approaching with care, I placed a light hand on her shoulder and offered a smile.

"Can I just get a minute of your time, Petula?"

"Oh, Stevie," she moaned, her lower lip quivering. "Everything's such a mess, and I think it's all because of Pascal. This is all my fault."

Tucking my purse under my arm, I gave her another gentle smile. "That's not true, Petula. All you did was hire one of France's best pastry chefs, whom you just happened to fall in love with. The heart gets in the way of the brain sometimes, that's all. Don't beat yourself up about this."

"I just don't understand how he had all this time to run around behind my back! I knew I should have hired Henri instead. What was I thinking?"

"Henri? Who's Henri?" No one had ever mentioned an Henri.

"Henri Prideux. He was the first pastry chef I interviewed, a perfectly lovely, fat, jolly man who was just as qualified as Pascal. But did I pay any attention to that? No. I was too busy swooning over Pascal's handsome good looks and charm. I behaved like an absolute schoolgirl and now look what's happened!"

"I had no idea you'd even entertained hiring anyone else, Petula." My astonishment was hard to hide.

Her red-rimmed eyes narrowed and her chapped lips flexed into a thin line as she let out a disgusted huff. "That's because I'm an old fool. Pascal is fifteen years my junior, for pity's sake. I don't know what I was thinking, but now that my ridiculous romance haze is clearing, I see very clearly the mistake I made."

I wanted to tread delicately here because Petula was so hurt, but something had been nagging me since the two of them had gotten together.

"About Pascal. Absolutely no offense, but I always wondered why someone so acclaimed would come to small-town Eb Falls all the way from France. He was always telling us about how he made pastries for all manner of royalty and suddenly he's willing to create his lighter-than-air confections for the bingo club? It made me question what brought him here."

Petula blew a breath of air, her cheeks puffing outward, the guilt in her eyes crystal clear. "I guess it doesn't matter if I tell you because it's going to get out

149

anyway, and it's not like the police told me to keep quiet about it…"

My ears burned, but I held my tongue and waited for Petula to speak.

"He was a filthy fake! That's what brought him here to Washington. He's no more French than I am a runway model," Petula spat.

I cocked my head to the left in question. "Say again?"

"Pascal's real name is Jerry Manzo, and he's not from France, he's from New Jersey. Piscataway, if I recall."

Holy cats! "So the French accent, the *oui oui* and croissants…?"

Her nose scrunched up in disgust. "All a total fake! I didn't find out until this morning, when the police told me his true identity. I'm sick about it, Stevie. I fell for it hook, line, and sinker. The only thing he was telling the truth about was he *does* have training as a pastry chef. He didn't go to school in France, but his credentials are real, for all the good that does anyone. An egotistical, lying pastry chef with a checkered past."

I blinked, almost unable to process this information. "And his wife?"

Petula's sigh was ragged. "He doesn't have a wife. He has a loan shark. That's who he was talking to on the phone that night I heard him. He came here to Eb Falls from New Jersey because he owed some loan shark money. So he stole some poor dead chef's name and became Pascal Le June. His fingerprints were in the police database. That's how they ID'd him. Because he isn't just a shyster, he's got a long history of wooing women with his Frenchness and stealing their money."

So we had another suspect, maybe? A loan shark. I pulled Petula into a hug and clenched my eyes shut. My heart ached for hers. I hated that she'd been duped.

"Oh, Petula. I'm so sorry."

She shuddered against me, but she sounded stronger than she had in Strange Brew, and that gave me hope. It was as if confronting Cassie had helped her push toward the road to empowerment.

"Bah!" she hissed. "Better I find out now than after he took off with my money, right? I knew something wasn't quite right about him wanting me to invest money so he could open his own shop in Seattle, but I was just so blinded by his good looks. I'm such an old fool."

Setting her from me, I brushed her mussed hair from her cheek. "No! That's not true. You have a good heart and you're a smart woman. Now, no more beating yourself up about it, understood? I won't have it."

Her return smile was grim, but Petula was a tough broad. She'd pull up her bootstraps and recover from Chef Bed Hopper in no time flat. I had faith. She'd built her business from the ground up all on her own; she'd rebuild her love life just the same way.

"I hate to brush you off, but I really have to go, Stevie. I've got to help search for Edmund. Is there anything else I can help with?"

"Just a couple more quick things. I know you said last night you didn't have any answers, but I thought maybe after having some time to talk with your staff and think things over, you might have remembered something. Do you have any idea why *Jerry* was at my house instead of Edmund last night?"

"If I had the answer to that, we might have another piece of this puzzle. None of us know why that lying thief went to your house. None of it makes any sense."

Dang. I just couldn't get a break. "Okay, and any idea why he'd leave such a nice note to me along with that special pastry? In all truth, he wasn't exactly the type of man to be so considerate."

Petula's eyes went wide in surprise as she placed her hands on her rounded hips. "Special pastry? What kind of pastry? What did it look like?"

"Uh-huh. Believe me, I was just as surprised. The note said it was an opera cake. I've never heard of it before, and of course, it struck me as odd he'd make something so delicate and what appeared to be incredibly time-consuming. Especially for me. It came off as so random."

Pressing her fingers to her lips, her brow furrowed as her gaze grew sheepish. "Opera cake, you say? I can't say I've ever heard of it, but I don't recall him making anything other than what you ordered, or writing you a note. What do you wanna bet he found out you were rich and decided to add you to the notches on his bedpost. He didn't just hook me with his good looks and French accent; he really was the quintessential pastry chef. Not that someone as smart and pretty as you would ever fall for such a bunch of hooey anyway. You just leave the stupid to us old broads."

"*Petula*," I warned, my smile admonishing. "No more of that. You're beautiful and smart and the best party planner/caterer in the business. Also, I adore you, and no one speaks ill of someone I adore. Not even the someone I adore."

No sooner had I spoken those words than the door of the shop blew open and Detective Kaepernick breezed inside, her ear to her cell.

"Yep. Got it, Boss. Asphyxiation and some unidentifiable plant substance we can only find one obscure mention of on the Internet. I'll get right on it and start asking questions," she barked—then paused and nodded, then frowned. "It's *what* you say?"

I knew I was eavesdropping, but I couldn't help leaning into the space between Melba and myself. If her conversation had to do with Chef Liar Liar Pants On Fire's cause of death, I wanted to hear.

But it was her next question that left my hands like icicles and struck terror in my heart.

"*Witches*? What does a rare plant from New Zealand have to do with witches, Boss?"

CHAPTER 11

"Oh, dear heaven," Win muttered.

I nodded in silent agreement. *You said it, buddy.*

Melba nodded her head and frowned again, driving a hand into the pockets of her jeans. "Right-right. Gotcha. Ah. I see. So there was a trace of this plant in the pastry and in the crumbs on the chef's mouth." Then she nodded animatedly. "Ahhh. Okay, so that wasn't what killed the dude, huh? Interesting-interesting. So you want me to ask what's in this opera cake?" She nodded again, her colorful hair with a fresh headband holding the bun atop her head in place bouncing about as she did. "Right. So keep the crazy witch stuff on the down low so people don't think we've plain lost our gourds. Can do."

Arkady whistled long and low. "This is no good, petunia. No darn good."

No. No, it wasn't good, and I had to figure out what it all meant.

It was then Melba realized we were all staring at her, her eyes rising to meet mine. Biting her lips, she winced before she returned to her call. "I've got that all now, sir. Yep. Sure-sure. I'll get right on this."

The silence in the room as Melba clicked the phone off, the various mouths of Petula's staff open in shock, made me feel badly for this new detective I was growing fonder of by the second. She was new to this detective business. It was plain to see she was incredibly eager and excited about her new job, despite Starsky's wet-blanket criticisms.

So she'd let the cat out of the bag. It wasn't that big a deal, was it? We were all going to find out how Chef Fake died eventually, right?

How he'd died made me pause, though. If I was hearing her correctly, this plant from New Zealand hadn't killed him? Well, that kind of threw a monkey wrench into my "poison Stevie," didn't it?

Melba's humiliation, steeping in that silence, set me into action. I reached for her arm and grabbed her hand, giving it a solid shake. "So good to see you again, Detective Kaepernick! How's detectiving? Are you settling into Eb Falls? Need any advice on where to get the best produce?"

Pulling her away from the crowd of people gathered, I continued to talk until we were in the niche by the kitchen doors.

"Aw, jeez Louise. I pretty much blew that sky-high,

didn't I?" She used her fingers to depict her words, flicking them in the air before splaying them apart.

I made light of her predicament and nudged her playfully. "Nah. Mistakes happen, Detective Kaepernick. Just ask Sandwich. He makes 'em with *me* all the time."

She snorted a laugh, putting her wrist over her mouth before recovering. "Still, I'm not supposed to be handing out information so sensitive like it's Halloween candy. It just caught me off guard, it was so weird."

"You mean the bit about the witches?" I asked, with the hope I came off vaguely intrigued rather than truly invested.

"Yeah-yeah. That makes no sense. The crumbs around the chef's mouth tested positive for some rare plant that—get this—witches use mixed with strands of baby's hair and something else I can't remember to make a poisonous spell or some such nonsense. Spooky-kooky, right? I don't even know how forensics found it. Someone's Google-Fu is strong, for sure. Maybe it's that guy Kip in Seattle? He's into all sorts of weird voodoo stuff." She shrugged and rolled her eyes, dismissing the idea. "Anyway, it's the only explanation anyone can find for why he'd have traces of it in his system. Sound's batty, right? I mean, spells? Crazy-nuts."

"So the pastry was tampered with? Told you, didn't I?"

I winked conspiratorially even as my stomach

plunged to my feet. Was this what Bel had meant by the cake?

Melba's eyes became shiny with more excitement then. "Even if it was tampered with—which is nuts if we start chalking stuff up to witches—that's not what killed him anyway. The plant just showed up in his tox report and Kip got a little overzealous when he went fishing for its uses on the web. The captain was just laughing about how crazy the witches and spells sounds, is all."

So the police were going to call no poison? Huh. "Then what actually killed Pascal?"

"Asphyxiation. Someone crushed his windpipe."

I gave a small gasp of horror I didn't mean to escape my lips. "*He was choked to death?* But I don't remember him having any marks on his neck when I saw him." It had been dark, but that still meant I'd missed something crucial. That also meant I still wasn't separating my emotions from my observations. I'd been so wrapped up in the mess my house was in and Bel's disappearance, I'd clearly missed a crucial clue.

Melba confirmed I wasn't the only person to miss the marks on his neck. "To be honest, we didn't see it either, but it was pretty dark. Postmortem revealed a lot. Looks like he was dragged and that's what killed him. Somebody's arm around his neck, they think. Cutting off his oxygen is what did him in."

I nodded my head in understanding, even though my stomach was a wreck. "And we still don't have any explanation for why he was in my house, do we?"

Melba popped her lips. "Nope. We're still trying to piece his movements from that day together."

"So I guess you're here to ask Petula about the plant? Search the kitchens, maybe? Figure out who made that pastry? Or does any of that matter when the cause of death was something else entirely?"

The ping of Melba's phone indicated she'd received a text. I waited while she glanced at the screen, my mind racing with all sorts of possibilities.

I wasn't convinced Pascal wasn't poisoned. Not even a little. Sure, the police would chalk up an obscure fact like whatever Kip found to a crazy, totally unscientific theory, but I knew better. They could and likely would dismiss the idea of a poisoning because the research brought up a witch's spell, but I couldn't. Not when witches were involved.

And in all seriousness, were a bunch of guys from forensics going to whip up this concoction of a spell and test its theory to see if it really did kill someone? I'm guessing not. This wasn't the same as testing blood spatter patterns or blunt force trauma.

But what if asphyxiation really was the cause of death? Where did that leave all our theories then?

"Everything okay?" I asked, peering over her shoulder to catch a glimpse of what was on her phone screen.

She nodded, her mouth set in a grim line as she stuffed the phone in the pocket of her jacket. "Yeah. Just a picture and some info on this crazy plant I have to ask about as a just in case. It seems kinda weird the pastry would have a rare plant in the recipe. All the research I did on this opera cake didn't call for any plants, but that could just be residue from the chef's fingers. It could be explained all sorts of ways."

Sure. It could be explained all sorts of ways, except why would the chef have the residue of a rare plant from New Zealand on his hands and why would he put it in a pastry for *me*?

I crossed my fingers Win or Arkady had caught sight of the picture before she'd tucked her phone away so we could investigate.

Lifting my eyes, I caught Melba's gaze again. "Still can't believe someone would kill the chef."

But Melba was clearly done sharing her information so freely. Stiffening up, as though she again realized she'd gone too far, the good detective gave me a curt nod. "Listen, I gotta get to work, Miss Cartwright. Thanks for makin' me feel better about all this. I've already said too much, but I appreciate your efforts nonetheless. If I don't see you before Christmas, have a merry." She raised a distracted hand and was off to question Petula, who still stood stunned and rooted to the spot I'd left her in.

She was in good hands with Melba. I knew that instinctively. The other half of Eb Falls' newest crime-fighting detective duo had grit, but she also had heart.

On my way out, I stopped Joanna Barnsworth, one of Petula's staff, and smiled at her. "Would you please tell Petula to call me if she needs anything—anything at all?"

She nodded her glistening blonde head. "Will do, Miss Cartwright."

I made my way back out into the rain, still stunned by this poison thing. Back in my car, I didn't know where to turn next. "Win, please tell me you got a look at Melba's phone," I groaned.

"I did indeed. It was a picture of one *Pennantia baylisiana*, considered the rarest plant or tree on Earth by the Guinness Book of World Records. Found off the coast of New Zealand at Three Kings Island."

"New Zealand," I crowed, still shocked by that piece of information. "And on its own it's not deadly. You know what that means, right?"

"I do not, Stephania. I'll admit, I'm quite stumped here."

But I wasn't. I saw where this was going. "The actual tree they found traces of might not be poisonous, but let me tell you, I know witches and how creative they can get when mixing potions for spells. I'm betting whatever this guy Kip Googled isn't so farfetched. He must've found some obscure reference to it online. Melba said he was into stuff like that, and of course everyone thinks the connection he made is plain nuts. They're humans. Humans don't believe we exist. Kip wouldn't be the first to run into something never meant for human eyes. Bel could tell you all about the time a witch got her hands on—"

I stopped myself and swallowed hard, cursing the threat of more tears. Talking about the good times I'd had with Bel hurt.

"Oh, *malutka*. Were I there with you, I would give you big polar bear hug," Arkady sympathized, using his mixed-up Russian take on American expressions.

"I know you would, and I'd polar bear hug you right back. But hugging won't get Bel back here with us where he belongs. I can't lose sight of that and get caught up with my emotional attachment to this case."

"Then this leaves us two options with regard to how that cad had a rare plant in his system, Stephania. One, Jerry knows a witch. The chances of that are about as likely as him being a personal acquaintance to the Queen, I'd suspect. Two, that pastry truly was meant for you. I don't understand how the chef became caught up in this, but we must now proceed with extreme caution."

I sat very still, shaken to my core. I was definitely the intended mark. "It's just like I said, what better way to ruin my best Christmas ever than to kill me with something sweet?"

"Precisely, Dove. I cannot for the life of me figure out how he made this pastry, but if this Adam knows anything about you, he knows you can't resist sweets. 'Twas you who ate fried Twinkies for dinner just last week, was it not?"

"Oh, hush, Judgy McJudgerson. I was busy decorating. I didn't have time to stop and make a proper meal. But this theory still doesn't explain how the chef got caught up in this. Why was he at the house instead of Edmund and why was he eating my pastry?"

"I'm still working on that," Win assured me.

All of this meant I'd gotten too comfortable after my last encounter with Adam. I'd hoped my mother had shipped him off to parts unknown, but the rare plant connected to a poisonous spell all said differently. Adam was still out there somewhere, trying to kill me, and I had absolutely no way to prevent that with no magic.

"Come, Stephania. It's time to go home and give this some thought. Whilst we scour the Internet for this spell, you must replenish your energy. You'll be no good to Bel half-starved and exhausted," Win chastised in a gentle tone.

The day was gray in Eb Falls, dark and gloomy, making the lights decorating each store twinkle with a Christmas glow. As I started the car, scanning the horizon over the Puget, the fear I'd never find Bel, that we'd never share another Christmas again, fought to consume me.

Win was right. Going home was the smartest thing I could do at this point. My energy levels were depleted, my heart deflated. Seeing Whiskey would help me regroup.

"Then home it is," I whispered.

~

I'd come home to a much simpler but equally beautiful Christmas lights display. As promised, Enzo and his crew had come over and removed all remnants of the debacle of last night and replaced everything but the nativity, which was still a crime scene, with lights in red and white strung for every peak and bough.

He'd also built Strike a hut right off the porch so he could come and go as he pleased, a beautiful new place for him to rest his head, with a heater and a trough for food and water. He and the boys had even cleaned up the parlor debris and stood the tree back up, turning it around so the missing branches weren't as visible. He'd brought in an entire team of people just for me.

Gratitude and the raw ache of Bel's absence had me crying like a baby on Enzo's shoulder, and he'd awkwardly thumped me on the back and let me sob it out in gulps for air and a runny nose.

The police had come and gone, searching the gardens and surrounding areas with their fine-tooth combs, leaving my lawn and porch a mess of muddy footprints and crime scene tape.

I had to wonder if they'd find any other footprints but those of mine and the judges.

Now, I sat in the kitchen and toyed with the bowl of soup Enzo had heated for me before he left, insisting he needed to see food in front of me, or Carmella would have his head.

I'd looked up the reference Melba mentioned. In fact, I found it rather easily. But the spell I found was incomplete. The spell Kip found online called for ground tree leaves mixed with a strand of baby's hair and a dash of ground agrimony. But that wasn't deadly at all.

None of the ingredients listed meshed with anything I'd ever been taught. So I emailed my good friend Winnie back in Paris, and that's how I found out when this plant was mixed with valerian root and a dash of turmeric—along with the strand of baby hair—it creates a powerful poison that, once in your blood-stream, stops your organs entirely.

Surely, they weren't going to take Kip's findings seriously. If I knew a whole stationhouse full of skeptical humans, I knew they'd sweep this right under the carpet. They had a perfectly logical explanation for Pascal's death—asphyxiation. I was pretty sure they'd stick with that.

In fact, I surmised, the only reason they had Melba investigate the plant was to shut this Kip up so he didn't make them all look crazy. I'd be surprised if the plant finding even ended up in the final report.

But that didn't change the fact that Pascal had been choked to death—by someone.

"Please eat, my daffodil. You must stay strong," Arkady encouraged.

"He's right, Dove. If there's one thing I can tell you as a former spy, your strength is imperative."

Pressing the heel of my hand to my forehead, I stared down at the rich broth with thick homemade noodles and chunks of tender chicken, but I couldn't summon the will to eat it when each spoonful sat in my stomach like lead.

"Anyone have any new ideas on this asphyxiation? I've been racking my brain, trying to come up with anything that could explain the chef being here, but I keep coming up dry."

"*Nyet*," Arkady whispered. "I am pained I have not been able to help. Give me a good interrogation, and I am the boss. But this...this with all its loose connections and speculation, has Arkady Bagrov stumped."

"Don't feel bad, old chap. It has Crispin Alistair Winterbottom stumped, too."

"Your name is *Crispin?*" Arkady crowed with schoolboy delight. "Crispin? How is it I do not know this, Crispy?"

Win chuckled. "Because spies don't tell their enemies their real names, Arkady Bagrov, a.k.a. JR Ewing Stepanov."

My favorite Russian spy gasped. "You know this sensitive information how, Crispy? It is top secret of highest priority!"

"You're real name is—is—JR Ewing *Stepanov*, Arkady? Like, the *Dallas* JR oil magnate Ewing?" Even in my misery, that made me snicker.

"Bah, my mother, a good Russian chicken farmer, she love the American television, especially the soap operas. When she give birth to me, he is popular on the TV."

My head fell back on my shoulders as I howled with laughter until tears ran down my face. The first genuine chuckle I'd had since Bel went missing. And then we all laughed until I think we each realized Belfry's tiny chuckle wasn't mingled with ours the way it had been for many months now—until we all realized *he* would have belly-laughed at Arkady's real name, too.

We each went silent at once, proving nothing would ever be right without Bel. I had to excuse myself from the table then, my tears blinding me as I made a run for the front door. I needed air, space, something to ease this ache and help me think.

Whiskey followed close on my heels, his small pants echoing in my ears as I hit the front steps of the porch and inhaled. "Beeelfryyy! Where are you, my friend? Talk to me! Please, *please* talk to me!" I screamed into the rush of bitterly cold wind.

The silence, filled only with the hard patter of rain and the crash of waves from the Sound, made me angry as tears of frustration welled in my eyes and poured down my face.

Slipping to the steps, I didn't care that it was pouring or that the temperature had dropped, I plopped down right on one of me and Bel's favorite spots—as though sitting there would make him suddenly appear because I wished it so.

We sat on these steps all summer long, watching the boats bob in Puget Sound, throwing a ball to Whiskey, sharing a glass of pomegranate juice because it was his favorite. We'd laughed over how much our lives had changed since I'd lost my powers.

We'd talked about our old friends back in Paris, Texas, smiled in gratitude over the new friendships we'd made since we'd moved back home to Eb Falls. We'd handed out candy to the children in the neighborhood who were brave enough to make the long walk up our driveway on Halloween.

We'd plotted my Christmas decorating coup right here on this step, laughing at how different this holiday would be surrounded by family and friends, compared to our past Christmases spent dining on Cheez Whiz and Bel's favorite, of all things, fruitcake.

And now it was just Whiskey and I out here on the steps. Whiskey, who nuzzled his wet nosey way under my arm and moaned a soft sigh, his longing for his buddy clear. In times like this, when I was afraid and lost, I did what I'd always done since I'd met Win. I reached out to him, seeking only the comfort he could bring.

"Win? You there?" I asked, looking up at the inky-black sky with its smoky-gray clouds.

"Yes, Dove. Always."

"I miss him so much," I croaked, my words hitching. "I'm so afraid for him. What if he's cold? Hungry?"

Win's presence was like a soft whisper across my cheek. "Oh, sweet Dove. What can I do to ease this pain? If I could take Bel's place, I would. Though we've only known each other a short time, know that he is as dear to me as anyone."

"What if...what if we never find Belfry?" I sobbed out his name, wrapping my arms around my waist and leaning forward to keep from falling apart.

The idea was unthinkable, but if I didn't let it out—at least voice my fears—I'd explode.

"Never is unacceptable."

"I'm terrified, Win. I'm so terrified. My life…I don't know where I'd be if not for Bel. He kept me going when I didn't think I could go anymore. He's all I had as a child. He kept me moving in the right direction. He loved me when my mother couldn't. He's everything to me. *Everything.*"

"Dove, listen to me, please. I beg of you. No matter how long, no matter what it takes, I will find our man Belfry and return him to you."

I wrapped my arms around Whiskey's neck and hugged him close, inhaling the scent of his damp fur and the cold night air enveloping us. "I wish you were here, Win."

Win's warmth surrounded me, hugging me tight. "As do I, my dove. As do I."

CHAPTER 12

"*A*re we ready?"

"Do you have cigar cutters, *malutka*? The wire snips?"

"Knock it off, JR. I already told you, no torture." I chastised Arkady with a roll of my eyes. "We're not torturing anyone because we don't know that we're going to come across anyone worth torturing."

"And surely you know by now, the church Christmas Eve gathering is no place for cigar cutters, old man. It's a church, for bloody sake. No violent interrogation accoutrement. Have some respect."

"I am just saying you do not catch a killer with flies. You must use vinegar," Arkady drawled.

I stuffed my wallet into my purse, wincing when I saw the scarf Belfry always tucked himself into whenever we went out. "That's honey, Arkady. And there will be no violence. We're just scoping the room, watching everyone, especially those yoga women's husbands. It's just like we talked about. Someone choked Chef Le June. Even thought we're fairly sure Adam is responsible for the poison in the pastry, and Chef ate it by mistake, it still makes no sense he'd choke the man, too. We're missing a link here. So maybe one of the Downward Facing Dog husbands found out about Pascal and they're responsible for offing him. Now, we have next to nothing in the way of evidence or proof and we're grasping at straws, but doing nothing was going to drive me absolutely crazy."

We'd spent late into the night last night and almost all day today theorizing and talking things out, and we continued to come up empty. I had no idea where Bel was, no idea if Adam truly had killed Pascal or whether he was even responsible for the fiasco at my house. I only had my gut.

But if he was, I had to keep my guard up. If Adam was involved, he wasn't your average human. In fact, he'd be even less easy to spot—a great concern for the spies in my life. For lack of anything else to do at this point, other than worry myself sick, we'd decided I should attend the Christmas Eve party as planned and see what I could see.

The folks of Eb Falls had planned a candlelight vigil for Edmund at midnight, after the church potluck supper. I was going to be there not only to show my support for Edmund, but to look for any clues to Pascal's killer.

I didn't want to be here. I didn't want to put on a pretty Christmas dress and smile at my friends and celebrate the holiday. But if anyone knew something, if anyone was hiding anything, I wanted to be the first to catch them at it.

"Okay, guys, let's do this. Arkady, you take the left of the room, Win, the right, and I'm front and center. Eyes and ears open."

"To war!" Arkady shouted his battle cry.

"Oh, stuff it, chap. No war cries. This isn't a battle. It's merely a fishing expedition. So behave yourself. No trying out your newly acquired ghost skills. Tonight's not the night."

As I made a break for the church steps, the steeple above me alight, I pondered. "Wait. Ghost skills? What have you been up to, Arkady? You know you have to be careful, right?"

"Bah! No worries, my peppermint candy cane. I am no threat. Not yet, anyway," he said, alluding to the fact that he was working on becoming a threat. Which worried me to no end.

"Tell that to the poor bloke who came to fix the heating vent last week while Super-Spy was practicing his wall-writing."

I stopped in the middle of the parking lot and looked around before I asked, "You can write on walls now?"

"Only in Japanese," he dismissed, as though knowing Japanese was no big deal. "It is okay. I erase before he blink his tiny eyes. He think this in his head."

"Which was the very reason he made an appointment at the neurologist's the next day, friend. You made him think he was seeing things," Win accused in their chummy way.

"No wall-writing, Arkady. No opening and closing doors. No flickering of the lights, just observation. Promise me."

"*Dah, dah.* I hear this loud and clear. It is a promise."

Satisfied we had a grip on our mission, I ran up the wide concrete steps, passing planters filled with red silk poinsettias and pushed my way through the double doors, only to run right into Enzo and Carmella.

"There she is!" Enzo called out from the wide foyer brimming with people. "Pretty as a picture. How you doin' today, gal?" He twirled me in a circle as Carmella chuckled.

I wrapped both he and Carmella in a hug, lingering in their warm vanilla-scented comfort. "Better, thank you. And thank you for what you did yesterday—you and the boys. You can't know what it means to have come home to those lights after yesterday, Enzo. You're really too good to me."

He flapped a hand at me and shook his head. "Nah. It wasn't nothin', kiddo. Just can't stand to see you sad."

"Don't you look pretty?" I said, rubbing Carmella's arm. I loved her abundant, soft warmth dressed in a red dress with a flouncy skirt and capped sleeves.

Carmella cupped my cheek, her round face filled with sympathy. "How are you, honey? I'm sorry about the chef. Next year, you let me teach you how to make cookies for those crabby judges. We'll fix their fancy pants up right and nobody'll end up dead. Promise."

I squeezed her wrist and smiled back, trying to keep my tears at bay. I was so grateful for these people. "It's a date."

Enzo nodded his head, flashing the red knit cap he wore in place of his baseball cap. "Well, c'mon then. We gotta get in there and see how we can help. Oh!" He paused, driving his hand into his sports coat pocket. "Found this when we were cleanin' up. Figured it fell outta somethin' of yours, kiddo."

He pulled out a tiny heart-shaped sapphire in a small Ziploc bag that looked like it belonged in a piece of jewelry, the sparkle of the gem under the lights capturing my full attention.

I plucked it from his fingers and held it up to the light. "That's not mine, Enzo, but it's beautiful, don't you think?"

"Well, I'mma guy," he explained. "It ain't beautiful unless it's round and shaped like a baseball," he said with a grin.

Carmella swatted him with her gloves but followed up with an indulgent smile. "Men! C'mon, Mr. Romantic. Pastor Fellows needs help in the kitchen with the stove. The back burner's not working."

I waved to them, tucking the stone into a small compartment in my purse before pulling off my coat and hanging it on one of the hooks in the entryway.

As I milled about, I noted the mood was quite somber compared to the past Christmas Eve events I'd attended when I was a child. The general chatter I heard as I passed groups of people said, while Edmund wouldn't want the children to miss out on the festivities of Christmas Eve, his absence was duly noted and wouldn't go without some kind of mention.

I made my way to the buffet table, listening to the hush of conversation, hearing the squeals of the children dressed in their Sunday best as they chased each other around the meeting room.

Mrs. Vanderhelm caught my gaze from the end of the buffet, her eyes avoiding mine as she turned her nose up at me then turned her back.

Good gravy. You'd think I purposely set out to ruin her day by deliberately leaving a dead chef in my nativity scene.

"Bah! That woman is sour raisins. It is no wonder she has no one to keep her warm on cold night. You ignore her, my pretty pound cake."

I fought a giggle and whispered as the room continued to fill up with familiar faces from town. "Anything yet?"

"Not yet, but we never give up boat!" he encouraged.

The weight of our situation kept threatening to drag me under, but knowing Win and Arkady were supporting me helped, so I kept strolling and listening.

Frank Morrison and Hank Winkowsky were busy stabbing their plates of sweet-and-sour meatballs with toothpicks, thinking no one saw them ogling Ralph Acres's wife and her curvaceous backside as she bent over his wheelchair and hand-fed him a cracker with cheese.

She really was gorgeous, so sleek and chic in her fitted white sleeveless dress with ice-white sparkling heels. Her blonde hair was up in a neat twist at the back of her head and her makeup was perfection.

Yep. I'd definitely call jealous on behalf of the Downward Facing Dog ladies. Not only was Patty Acres at least five years younger than they were, she was a hundred times more gorgeous.

I'd meant to drop by the hospital yesterday to see if Ralph was feeling better, but ended up sending flowers in lieu of visiting, to concentrate all my efforts on Bel's disappearance.

Now I realized I at least needed to offer him another apology for essentially breaking his leg—even if I did end up saving his life. I mean, he could have eaten a contaminated pastry meant for me.

But I guess I couldn't tell him that. I wasn't even sure if the news Pascal had died of asphyxiation was out yet.

On a deep breath, I threaded my way through several parishioners and gave Ralph a sheepish wave just as Patty went back toward the buffet table to gather another plate. He didn't look half bad, and that pleased me no end. His cheeks were rosy and his eyes bright.

"Hi, Ralph. How are you feeling?" I asked with a smile.

He gave me a wary look, the red undertone of his skin going redder. "I only have two legs, Stevie Cartwright, and I can't afford to have another one of 'em broken at my age. You stay back there." He pointed a knobby finger to the far end of the room and shooed me.

If there's ever another Christmas Lights Display Contest, I think I'm going to lose by default as the leg breaker.

I held up two hands as white flags. "Again, I'm so sorry, Ralph. It was a total accident, but I've notified the billing department at Eb Falls General to send me the entire bill. I'll take care of everything. Promise."

But his face didn't lighten up in quite the way I'd hoped, and I suppose that was fair enough. I mean, "hey, I broke your leg but I'll pay for everything" hardly seems like much compensation when you end up in a wheelchair.

Ralph waved his finger at me again, his face screwing up as he shifted in his wheelchair, the leg with cast propped up by a green and red pillow. "That's mighty fine of ya. Thank you kindly. Now go away."

"Oh, Ralph! Don't be rude and so grudgy! Stevie explained it was an accident," Patty pointed out as she came up behind me and gave my shoulders a light squeeze.

My nose twitched, jogging something in my brain I couldn't put together, but I patted her hand and nodded in earnest. "It really was, Ralph. Honest. I still don't even know what happened to my decorations, but I never meant to hurt you. I would never do something like that on purpose. Surely you know that."

"Of course she wouldn't, Ralph, and you know

that's so," Patty said with a tap to my shoulder before she moved from behind me to stand next to Ralph's wheelchair.

As she placed a protective hand on her husband's shoulder and the twinkling lights strung around the room hit her throat, the room tilted before righting itself again, giving me a very clear picture.

I almost gasped out loud. *No. No. That couldn't be.*

But it was. I knew it in my gut. I just didn't know how it all fit.

I fought for composure, fought to string words together that made sense before I opened my big mouth and said anything more. As the party went on around me, I formulated my thoughts.

"You all right there, Stevie?" Patty asked, her crystalline-green eyes mild with suspicion.

"Me?" I asked in fake surprise, stalling as my mind raced. "Oh, I'm fine. I was just wondering, what's the name of the scent you're wearing? I love it."

She winked and grinned, flashing her perfect white teeth. "My Ralph buys it for me. It comes directly from France. He spoils me so, don't you, honey?"

"It's lovely," I complimented, moving closer to peer at her neck. "Did you know you're missing a stone from your necklace, Patty?"

Her long fingers flew to her throat, where a strand of heart-shaped sapphires hung on a thick gold chain against her beautiful clear skin, and she gasped.

I popped open my purse and reached into the zippered compartment, pulling out the small gem. "You know, my friend Enzo found one just like it at my house yesterday, when he cleaned up the mess from the Christmas tree I knocked Ralph into. You've never been to my house, Patty. How do you suppose it got there?"

The look of shock on her face was matched only by the look on Ralph's.

"And that perfume from France? It's pretty distinct. I bet if I let Cassie Haverstock take a whiff of you, she'd tell the police it smells exactly like the perfume Chef Le June came to her house reeking of, now wouldn't she?"

"*Cassie?*" a male voice said, bewildered.

My eyes flew to the section of chairs behind Patty and Ralph—where Cassie's handsome husband Jack sat, a plate of baked ziti in his lap, his fork suspended midair.

"Cat's out of the bag, Stevie!" Win crowed. "Proceed with caution."

Shoot. I hadn't meant to say that out loud. But it created a roar in the crowd of people gathering as everyone began to chatter at once.

And as I began to put everything together, I moved in on Patty. "It was *you*, wasn't it, Patty?" I accused, pushing my way past the people standing between us. "You were having an affair with Chef Le June, too!"

What happened next is something I don't think I'll ever forget as long as I live.

Patty grabbed the handles of Ralph's wheelchair and made a run for the foyer toward the church doors, plowing through the crowd and screaming, "We're making a break for it, Ralph honey!"

Boy, I gotta hand it to her; she was really quick in those heels, crashing through the double doors with me in hot pursuit.

But the part I'll never forget? That Patty actually thought she could escape when the only way to do that was to push a wheelchair with a fully grown, very large man down a flight of thirty or so steps.

I saw the very top of Ralph's head just before both he and the wheelchair toppled down the steps with Patty clinging to the handles. The bounce and crunch of steel and the screech of Ralph hollering the whole way rang out in the parking lot.

The couple ended up in a crumpled heap on the sidewalk, Ralph flat on his back with Patty sprawled out partially underneath the spinning wheels of the chair.

"I see Stevie Cartwright's arrived," Dana Nelson whispered with a laugh as we both looked down the steps. "Never let it be said you don't know how to bring the fun, little lady."

CHAPTER 13

"So explain this to me again," Dana ordered, notepad in hand as Sandwich hovered over Ralph and Patty while they waited for a police car to arrive, and another one of the off-duty police officers kept the crowd from the church at bay.

"It wasn't her!" Ralph blustered, his red face growing redder by the minute as the pastor's wife covered him in a blanket, now that he'd been righted in his wheelchair. "Leave the wife alone! It was me! I take full responsibility for all of it."

"*You?*" I squeaked. I was still trying to figure out how someone like Patty had managed to drag the chef out into my nativity set—but I guess stranger things have been known to happen—when Ralph blurted out his confession.

Ralph sighed, moaning when he shifted in his wheelchair. "Yes, *me.* I found out Patty was foolin' around on me. So I was gonna confront him—you know, man to man. I got in my car and followed that dirtball to your house the day I found out about his affair with Patty. I don't know what he was goin' there for, I just know I was seein' all kinds of red and I wanted to smash his fancy face in!"

"But why were you at my house?" I asked Patty. I still just couldn't make the connection.

Her expression went from anguish to guilt in the matter of a moment. Pushing her mussed hair from her face, she rasped a sigh. "I was following Pascal because I was convinced he was cheating on me with someone else. I must've gotten to your house just after Ralph and Pascal arrived. When I saw Ralph's car in your drive-way…I knew I had to get in there before they tore each other apart," she sobbed softly.

So this had all been a series of crazy coincidences culminating in the death of Pascal? Holy cats. Still, why was the chef at our house to begin with and why did he eat the darn pastry? Had he read the note?

"What a bloody mess," Win mumbled.

"But I'm tellin' you, he was half dead when I got there, Stevie! You gotta listen to me!" Ralph shouted in a sudden burst of energy, grabbing at my hand. "He was on the floor, his face all ugly red with the crumbs from that pastry all over his face. It was the pastry that made him sick! You can't blame us for that! We had nothing to do with it. Patty can't even boil water!"

Patty nodded her head with a shiver, tightening her hold on the top of her torn dress. "It's true! I don't know how to cook, let alone bake something like that! It wasn't us, it was the pastry!"

Rubbing my arms to ward off the chill, I had to ask, "But how did he get outside, Ralph? Why would you leave him there like that?"

"Aw, heck. I tried to haul him up and get him to my car to take him to the hospital. I didn't even have my cell phone with me or I woulda called 9-1-1. But we never made it. He kept sputterin' and coughin' and then...he just..."

Patty bobbed her head, her hair falling in her eyes as tears streamed down her face, streaking her mascara. "It's true! He's telling the truth. Pascal was on the floor when I got there. We were just trying to help him, but he died. He died without any help from anyone! Ralph checked his pulse and he was gone."

"My heavens. Was there anyone in this town Jerry wasn't making hay with?" Win cracked.

But I waved my hand in the air to quiet him. "So you just left him in my nativity scene when you realized he was dead and didn't call the police for help?"

Ralph scrubbed a hand over his face and nodded in guilt, his misery plain. "We knew how it would look to everybody. It looked bad. Real, real bad. So we got scared and took off. There was nothin' we could do for the dirtball anyway. He was dead!"

"He's telling the truth!" Patty shouted in desperation as sirens blared in the distance. "We didn't kill him. I swear!"

"Then why didn't you at least say something when

Mrs. Vanderhelm found him, Ralph? You behaved as though you knew nothing! I was right there," I accused with a shiver. Boy, he'd played that well. I never once suspected he knew anything about what happened to Pascal.

Ralph groaned low in misery, pulling the blanket up around his chest. "I know it was stupid, but I spent too long in my head, Stevie, thinkin' about all the ways we could get blamed. We decided as a couple we were better off keepin' our mouths shut."

I used my finger to jab the air, waving it at Ralph. "Then why the heck would you try to eat one of the pastries? If you thought that's what killed Pascal, why would you even consider it?"

His shoulders sagged in defeat under his plaid sports coat. "Because when Patty went and looked at the pastry, the stone from her necklace must've fallen off and right into that cake. I noticed it while we were waitin' for the police to question us. Recognized it right away. I was just tryin' to get it out of sight so the police wouldn't call it evidence and connect it to Patty, but you knocked me over before I could get to it."

Aha. Now that part of the story did make sense. "And it fell off the pastry and onto the floor, where Enzo found it," I finished, not even paying attention to Ralph and Patty anymore.

Even though it still didn't explain how the pastry had gotten there in the first place, or the poison—yes, I was still convinced the pastry had been poisoned. But

I'd lay bets the police were going to find a way to cover up the tune Ralph and Patty were singing.

"We had nothing to do with that pastry. I don't know what was in it, but I bet that's what killed him! So you can't blame us for anything but not calling the police!" Ralph yelled.

Sighing, I shook my head at the irony of all this. "But Pascal didn't die because he ate the pastry, Ralph. He died because his airflow was cut off. I'm betting you wrapped your arm around his neck when you dragged him outside. That's what killed him."

"Nooo!" Patty cried out as Sandwich used a light grip to keep her near.

As the lights of an Eb Falls police car came into view, my heart began to race. Ralph was the last connection I had to Belfry, and I had to find out if he'd seen anything when he'd found Pascal.

But Dana moved to stand between Ralph and myself. "Stevie, we have to bring him in now."

Pushing Dana out of the way, I grabbed the arm of Ralph's wheelchair. I worked hard not to burst into tears when I asked, "Did you see anyone else at my house that day, Ralph? Anyone at all? Did you hear anything?"

"You mean besides that mess outside and that dog of yours barkin' like he'd lost his mind?"

"Yes! Was anyone else there? Anything strange?" I imagine I must've looked pretty intense, maybe even a little desperate, which clearly alarmed Ralph.

Without warning, Ralph appeared to realize whatever he said could incriminate him and he clammed up. "You'll just have to ask my lawyer. I'm not sayin' anything else."

Dana latched on to my arm and pulled me away from Ralph as Melba and Detective Moore rushed up the sidewalk. "Stevie? What's going on?"

Crossing my arms over my chest, I gazed up at him in his smart suit and tie, looking as dapper as he did in everything he wore. "Well, Officer Nelson, there are still a hundred unanswered questions I'd like some answers for."

Sucking in his cheeks, he gave me that half-indulgent, half-annoyed expression. "Like?"

Yeah, Stevie, like?

How could I ask him about the poison if the police weren't going to acknowledge it even existed? How could I ask him about that note, knowing with almost certainty Adam had written it?

Instead, I went for the obvious questions needing answers. "Like, why was the chef at my house to begin with? Like, where's Edmund? Like, who messed with my decorations? Don't you want to know the answers to those questions, too?"

Dana cocked a smile at me, his eyes playful. "Sure I do, Miss Cartwright. But I'm off duty, and you're not a police officer with the authority to ask those questions. We'll have to leave that to our fine Ebenezer Falls detectives."

Sighing, I had to recognize he was right. The rest of this mystery would have to stay under wraps because if they all thought I was crazy as a bedbug now, I can only imagine how they'd feel when I brought up poisonous witch spells and vengeful warlocks.

"Fine," I said with a roll of my eyes.

"You got your man—again. Why the fuss?"

The fuss? What's the fuss? My familiar's been kidnapped! That's the fuss. But I couldn't say that either, could I?

So I just shook my head and tried to keep my shrug nonchalant in order to downplay my desolation. "I guess I just want answers. I know I drive you all insane with my pestering, but you know a good mystery and me. I just can't resist."

Dana's eyebrow rose but he grinned and leaned down, dropping a quick kiss on my cheek. "You did it again, Wannabe Detective. Now, I have to go, Miss Cartwright, but if I don't see you, have a Merry Christmas."

Gulping, I patted his arm and managed a smile. "You, too, Officer Rigid."

His laughter mingled with the commotion going on around me and the astonished chatter of the party attendees, but I took no joy in figuring out this particular mystery.

Belfry was still missing and it was Christmas Eve.

And we were no closer to finding him than we'd been two days ago when he'd disappeared.

∾

*W*e made the ride home in silence. There were no high-fives for a mystery-solving well done. There was no joy in finding Pascal's killer, even if killing hadn't been what Patty and Ralph had in mind when they'd gone to my house that day.

I briefly wondered if some of the answers we sought, like why Chef had been there that day, would ever be answered, and then I closed my mind off to all of it.

Pulling into our driveway, I put the car in park and leaned back in the seat, clenching my fists tight.

"Dove…"

I shook my head as I battled tears. "Don't try to make this better, Win. You can't make this better! What are we going to do? I failed. I failed the best friend I've ever had. He's out there, all alone on Christmas Eve, and we have nothing. Less than nothing. No leads, no clues. He's just vanished and become a voice only I can hear. Tell me what to do! Because I don't know where to go from here!" I rasped out the words, the last of my patience stretched to impossible lengths.

I'd more than failed. I'd flopped. I'd flopped so hard.

"*Malutka*, please. Arkady Bagrov cannot bear your sadness. Let us go inside where it is warm and we will think some more. We are three heads. We will figure this out."

But I'd heard that more times than I cared to count

these past couple of days. I just couldn't hear it anymore.

And then I had an idea. If Adam was responsible for kidnapping Belfry, if his motive had been to ruin my best Christmas ever and kill me, he was watching me. Or he had someone watching me. If what Arkady had said the other day was true, then he was watching me right now.

The hunted was officially tired of being hunted, sick and tired of tiptoeing through life while she waited for the dirtbag warlock who'd stolen her life to take her by surprise.

No more.

Throwing the car door open, my rage, my frustration at an all-time high, I stumbled out onto the driveway just as sleet began to pour from the sky. "Adam! Adam Westfield—I compel you to make yourself known!" I screeched into the night, flying across the driveway and onto my soggy lawn, my arms open wide. "You want a piece of this? Come and get it, coward!"

"Stephania! Stop it! Stop it this instant!"

"No, Win. No more! No more living in fear. No more waiting and wondering. If that weakling wants a shot at me, stop playing games and come and get it, warlock!" I bellowed, punching the code to the front door into the security system app on my phone and shoving my way inside.

The house was dark but for the lights on the

Christmas tree, and still—so still, not even Whiskey came to greet me.

"Daffodil, you will listen to Zero and stop this behavior now! Arkady Bagrov begs you to keep mouth shut!"

"I won't watch that again, Stephania! I will not watch you be hunted!"

But I wasn't listening. Not anymore. If Adam Westfield wanted a fight, he was going to get one. A big, ugly, knock-down-drag-out fight.

Gritting my teeth, I ran back into the entryway and spread my arms wide, raising my eyes to the ceiling. "Adam Westfield! By the power of the coven, by the laws of Baba Yaga, I compel you to show yourself!" I roared, the echo of my words flying upward to the vaulted ceiling.

"Miss Cartwright?" someone squeaked in what sounded almost like disbelief.

Both Arkady and Win gasped just as I lowered my eyes and blinked. "Edmund? Oh, sweet Pete, Edmund, is that you?"

Sure as the day is long, Edmund stood in the entryway to the kitchen, still in his uniform from Petula's, shivering, dripping wet, with a puddle of muddy water forming at his feet.

"I'm so glad to see you, Miss Cartwright," he murmured, his words coming out choppy from his convulsive shivers.

"Oh, Edmund!" I called, my hands outstretched as I

raced toward him. "What happened to you? Where have you been?"

Just as I reached him—I mean the moment my feet stopped short in front of his—was the moment I realized my enormous mistake.

This wasn't Edmund. The eyes that stared back at me weren't shiny and kind. They were glassy and lifeless, almost zombie-like.

Well, technically it was Edmund. The shell of his body, anyway.

But the rest? The sudden murderous gleam in his chocolate-brown eyes, the flash of the biggest kitchen knife I owned?

That was all Adam Westfield.

CHAPTER 14

"Stevie, look out!" Win howled, just as Edmund reached for my hair, sinking his fingers into my scalp and dragging me toward him.

I tripped, falling to the ground and spinning around on my knees until my back was to him, thus, giving him the perfect opportunity to capture me.

Adam's fingers sank back into my hair, gripping it so hard, my scalp stung and burned.

"Let me go!" I cried as I struggled and made an attempt to jab at his ribs with an uppercut of my elbow, only to meet the sharp point of the knife he held at my ribs.

"Oh, no, no, no, my little ex-witch," he cackled, the soft edges of Edmund's voice totally gone, now replaced with the deeper, menacing strains of Adam's. "I'm never letting you go, Stevie. You're right where I want you after all this time."

"*Malutka*, you listen to Arkady! Go limp. Do not

fight. Let him drag you. Keep your body this way, so your back is to him, then when he least expects it—whammo! Right in his kissy face. Put your fists together and drive them upward into his nose!"

"Listen to Arkady, Dove! Bide your time."

I remembered this lesson, the go-limp theory. I think I'd even used it once before with a modicum of success. So I relaxed, letting Adam drag me trembling into the kitchen, past the island, the heels of my nylons tearing on the hardwood floor until we were at the kitchen table by the bay windows overlooking Puget Sound.

That was when the lights flipped on and I saw everything very clearly. So clearly, my heart jumped from my chest to my throat, pounding out a beat of sheer terror.

Bel hung in the middle of the kitchen from one of the pendant lights, a noose around him, fashioned to tighten around his tiny neck if disturbed. Whiskey...oh my poor, sweet Whiskey. He barked somewhere off in the distance from upstairs, his growl full of fear and anguish.

Dragging my head back even farther, Adam forced me to look up at Bel, shivering and small. "You make one wrong move and that noisy, overstuffed wad of useless cotton dies, hear me?" he whispered in my ear.

Yet, it was all I could do not to scream out Belfry's name in relief. Tears rushed to my eyes, falling down my face at how helpless he was, but I fought the urge to call out to him and focused on Adam and his simmering rage.

"Let him go and you can do whatever you want to me, Adam. Just let him go," I said with a calm that even surprised me. "He had nothing to do with what happened between us."

He gripped my hair harder, yanking my head back so far toward his chest, my neck ached from arching upward. "Didn't you hear, Detective Stevie? There's no negotiation here. There's no give and take. I've waited a long time for this moment. I planned. I practiced. I practiced hard to get this possession just right, and then I picked the perfect moment to execute. Your favorite holiday. You took everything from me, Stevie Cartwright, and now I'm going to take everything from you—and when your family shows up here tomorrow, they're going to find you dead. Just like my family found me!"

"Why?" I croaked, my throat on fire. "Why not just kill me and get it over with? Why the elaborate plan? Why the show?"

I'd learned a thing or two since murder had become a consistent part of my life. Most killers wanted a voice —to be heard. They enjoyed spelling out their motives, and talking over their meticulous machinations with their victims just before they dropped the hammer.

It was like murderer code or something.

Adam's breathing became rapid, his chest rising and falling in harsh rasps. "It's all a means to an end—a bitter end. What better way to make your last days on

Earth miserable than by taking everything you love at your favorite time of year, Stevie? It's poetic justice, don't you think?" he growled.

"The decorations, the phone calls changing all my plans, the turkeys. That was all you. And that pastry," I hissed out, the sound strained and harsh. "That was meant for me, wasn't it?"

Hauling me upward, Adam pressed his lips to my ear, sending a wave of revulsion through me. "Beautiful, wasn't it? It could have all been over then if Edmund here hadn't ruined everything by calling that chef to ask how it got there."

"Stephania, don't you dare..." Win warned, low and threatening.

Gosh, he knew me so well. Of course I was going to ask how the pastry got there. *"How did it get there?"*

Win's inhale was sharp in my ear. "Bah! Stephania, bloody well knock it off! Have you paid no attention to the shiny weapon this madman wields?"

Adam's cackle was cold, so cold and devoid of anything but hatred, I had to fight the tremors my body so wanted to expel.

"I possessed the chef at first, of course. His deft, lying, cheating hands helped me make it then I snuck it into your order and tucked the note away under the bottom layer of the pastries you ordered. What kind of sleuth are you if you couldn't even figure that much out? I'm a sad panda you didn't have the chance to taste it just before all that flaky crust and smooth custard shut down every organ in your body. Now that would have been delightful to see. Alas, things got sticky."

"*I will kill him with bare hands!*" Arkady roared so loud, it made me stop and wonder why Adam didn't appear to notice.

And then I remembered, because he'd possessed a human, his powers became dimmer on this plane.

I battled to speak, to keep Adam in a place where he thought he had the upper hand. "Okay so, too bad, so sad," I husked out, my throat growing raw. "I didn't eat the pastry. I see your crushing disappointment and raise it with a question—actually two. Why was the chef here?"

Securing the knife in his hand, he let the tip dig into my side with enough pressure to break the skin. "Oh, *that*," he said dryly. "He was certainly a jealous, egotistical man, that Pascal. Everything was going so smoothly. Edmund here uncovered your delicacy during setup, but he thought it strange the moronic chef had left you a pastry and a note, probably for the same reasons you did. So he called him up and that buffoon drove right over here to see what Edmund was making such a fuss over."

Click. Click. Click. Everything fell into place after that. Well, almost. Still trying not to fight the tide, I asked question number two. "But why did he eat it?

Adam chuckled, dry and rife with menace. "Because your chef couldn't believe someone other than him had created something so beautiful. He thought someone named Henri made the pastry. Naturally, he couldn't resist sampling the competition's artistry before I was done possessing Edmund to stop him. And then of course, you know the rest. That oaf of a man showed up with his brainless wife. Alas, it required a change of plans."

"Like kidnapping my familiar?" I gritted out.

Gosh, my back ached, the muscles along my sides were on fire. I'd been in spy training for months now, but there was still always a muscle or tendon I somehow missed in our workouts, and found out about when I was in the most precarious of positions.

He rubbed his cheek against the top of my head and sighed. "Ah, well, I needed a little time to work out a plan B, seeing as that nitwit chef ruined everything. Why not break your heart while I was at it? Your little friend's still alive—for the moment, anyway."

My fists clenched as Adam dragged me again, my body threatening to tense up as the instinct to fight back continued to grow stronger.

"Limp like cooked spaghetti, dill pickle. Do as Arkady says," he soothed, his words easing my wish to flee.

"So how is this all going to end, Adam? Where do we go from here?"

The knife he held in his free hand arced upward, catching the light in the kitchen as he backed up past the table and toward the laundry room door. "I slit your throat, Stevie Cartwright, and you bleed out all over the floor. I take from you just the way you took from me," he seethed. "*That's* how this goes."

Every muscle in his body tensed in tune with mine. The white-hot threads of his hatred for me seeped into my bones and made me clench my teeth.

"Limp, stay limp, Dove. Please," Win encouraged, his voice dredged in concern. "Just keep playing along."

"But wait! You took my powers in return! Do you remember that night, Adam? The night you slapped them out of me? I lost everything, too! I lost my friends and my home, my job, my entire life!"

"Can one really compare the two, Stevie? You lost some powers. I lost my *life!*" he screeched so loud, I think my bones rattled.

My breathing had become rapid now, too, the tension in my chest almost unbearable. And of course, that made me angry. I'd been attached to this warlock and his vengeance far too long.

"But you were a bad man, Adam—a bad, mean man! You abused your wife and son! You deserved to die!"

"*Shut up!*" he screamed, jerking me against him again, raising the knife once more until it hovered in front of my eyes. "Just shut up and prepare to die, Stevie Cartwright! See you on the other side!"

What happened next is rather a blur. I remember hearing Win call out, "Arkady—on three!" and feeling like the door to the laundry room sort of blew outward, knocking Adam into me with such force, we both fell to the floor.

The knife he'd threatened me with skittered across the hardwood, clattering against the cabinets and landing in the doorway between the dining room and the kitchen.

Then I remember the race was on to see who could get to the lethal weapon first. I was on my feet and launching myself at it in a moment's notice, grateful Win had taught me the value of kettlebell lifting—they did indeed keep a core strong.

I landed just shy of the knife as though I were sliding into home base just as Adam caught my ankle and began to drag me back toward him. Whiskey's frantic barks from upstairs became louder, his fear making my heart pound.

"Right heel to the jaw, Stevie!" Win bellowed, and I followed suit, taking great satisfaction in Adam's howl of pain.

"To your feet, *malutka*!" Arkady directed, making me scramble to get a foothold and make a break for it.

Yet, the moment I was on my feet was the moment Adam took me back down again, grabbing me around the waist and flattening me with a grunt.

We slammed into the floor with a bone-crunching crack, my face smashing against the hardwood, leaving me dazed. But somehow, even as my eyes rolled in my head like a slot machine, I managed to walk my fingers across the floor and locate the knife.

If I'd learned nothing else from my two favorite spies, I'd learned you could compartmentalize a certain amount of pain if you kept your eye on the prize— defeating your opponent.

"Don't let go of that knife, Dove!"

But Adam ground his body into my back, slipping his arm around my neck and latching on to the wrist of the hand that held the weapon. He yanked my forearm up toward him and twisted it at an awkward angle until I screamed out in pain, the sharp stab of white-hot agony making my eyes water.

But I anticipated his plan to wrest the knife from me by simply letting it go, the satisfying ping it made when it hit the floor music to my ears, as was his scream of rage when I drove that same hand upward and clocked him square in his face.

"Nice job, Dove!" Win cheered while Arkady whistled his approval.

His arm loosened around my neck upon impact, giving me the opportunity to brace both my palms against the floor and rear up, knocking him from me with a blood-curdling howl of my own rage.

And then I turned the tables, launching myself at him and flattening him against the floor. Scrambling to a sitting position, I straddled his waist and reached down to grab a handful of his curly hair, my eye on the knife just to the left.

I gave his head a good bounce against the hardwood, good enough that his eyes rolled to the back of his head, giving me enough time to latch back onto the knife.

"Beautifully done, *malutka!* Bravo!"

"I'll kill you!" he screeched, clawing at my hands with desperate fingers.

"Not before I kill you!" I screamed back, my heart a

heavy throb in my chest as I, without qualm, prepared to plunge the knife into his chest.

But it all ended there when Win cried out, "No, Stevie! You mustn't. You'll kill Edmund!"

Technicalities, technicalities, right? I'd forgotten about possession and the rules. Host bodies don't like it if you kill them.

Naturally, that was all it took for me to lose my killer-instinct focus and the tables turned once more. Adam flipped me so fast, I almost stopped breathing, and then his hands were at my neck.

Sweet, gentle, awkward Edmund was now red-faced, bulging-eyed killer Adam. As his hands wrapped around my neck and he began to squeeze, white lights flashed behind my eyes.

Win and Arkady screamed directions but I couldn't make out their words for the pounding of my heart as I bucked under him, heaving my hips upward to no avail. My hands went to Adam's wrists, clinging to them, tearing at them, and somehow I managed to loosen his grip, but only for a moment.

He latched back on to me by way of my necklace, gripping it and pulling it tight around my neck until I saw stars.

I knew unconsciousness was mere seconds away. I knew this was the end if I didn't do something—*anything.*

Which was why the rumble of thunder came as such a welcome surprise.

Just as Adam tore at my necklace, the room quaked

and rolled, forcing him backward with a jolt. When he ripped the chain from my neck, my flesh stung as it tore across my skin.

A flash of light sliced through the room, silhouetting Adam, his teeth clenched, his arm raised toward the ceiling, his fist balled so tight his knuckles were white. The strain of his muscles, the frozen agony on his face, lasted a split second before there was an explosion of color and a tendril of smoke.

Using my elbows, I forced myself upward, only to watch Adam collapse to the floor, his muscles finally relaxing and releasing as he crumpled in a heap of limbs.

I blinked as the moment remained suspended, while the silence settled.

And then Win called out, "Stephania!"

I held up a hand with a cough, getting my first whiff of the air that had grown so still. "I'm okay. Just give me a sec," I said, hauling myself to my knees.

"What was this that just happened before my very eyes?" Arkady asked, his disbelief lacing his words.

I couldn't help it. I laughed. Then I coughed because wow, Edmund was strong. "That was a little bippity-boppity-boo."

"The necklace!" Win shouted with a laugh. "The necklace your father gave you saved you?"

Reaching upward, I grabbed the island's counter and pulled myself up with a nod. "Yes. At least I think so. Do you remember when he said I should always wear it so he'd always be with me? Back when we had the housewarming?"

"I remember it well, Dove. It was a lovely moment for the both of you."

Rubbing my throat, I smiled. My dad was awesome, and I planned to tell him just that tomorrow. "He must've filled it with some kind of protection spell or something, because do you smell that?"

"Smell what?"

I wrinkled my nose, the musky scent of life and death still swirling in my nostrils. "A spirit. That smell is Adam's spirit leaving Edmund's body."

"I hesitate to ask, but does this mean he's gone for good, Dove?"

I heard the fear in Win's voice, the anger, but he wasn't going to like my answer. Inhaling, I shook my head. "I don't think so. But let's just be thankful for small favors at this point. Whatever my father put in that amulet will keep him at bay—for a while, anyway. To have pulled off that stunt had to have sapped his power. It'll be a while before we hear from him again." *I hoped.*

"What is this? You can smell spirit? He can possess bodies? Bah! I do not know how I feel about you Americans and your witches. This is crazy talk!" Arkady balked.

"Are you still disputing the existence of magic, JR? I have a funny feeling you know a little something about that. Wasn't it both you and Win who used your mojo to blow the laundry room door open, effectively knocking me out of harm's way?"

They both laughed in unison. "Bahahahaha! We are like Gorev and Gurkovsky!"

"Who?" Win squawked.

"Don't be silly, Zero," Arkady poo-pooed. "Everyone knows Gorev and Gurkovsky. They are greatest action movie stars from Russia!"

I giggled. "Well, listen, G and G, whatever you did stalled Adam, and it was awesome. But trust me, in the end, whatever my father put in that necklace saved my life."

"And Edmund?" Win asked, his tone going serious.

I looked to poor Edmund's slumped body. "He'll be fine. Thank goodness, he'll be okay. We're going to have to find some kind of explanation that appears plausible to everyone about his disappearance, but he's going to be okay."

"Amnesia? A drunken escapade?"

"Something that doesn't make him look irresponsible or sound like he's been doing time on a soap opera, Win." Brushing my hands together, I pushed off the island and made my way toward Edmund.

As I looked down at him, all I could think was, this poor, sweet boy. I was pretty sure he wouldn't remember any of this, not the possession or, I hoped, the violence.

Slipping my hands under his arms, I pulled him up to a sitting position when I heard, "Hey! Blood rushing to my head here!"

"Belfry!" I cried, setting Edmund down with gentle hands and grabbing one of the overturned kitchen chairs to climb up on the counter and reach the pendant light Bel swung from. My hands fumbled with the noose around his tiny neck until he was free and I could smother his tiny head with kisses.

"Yeah. Belfry," he said dryly. "You know, bat who got kidnapped and had harrowing experience?"

Pulling him close, I rubbed my cheek against his soft fur, tears slipping from my eyes. "Oh, Bel, I was so scared I'd never find you. I love you, buddy. Nothing is the same without you."

He nuzzled me back, burrowing against my ear. "I called you like a bazillion times, didn't you hear me?"

"I called back, but I guess you didn't hear me either. *Where* have you been?"

"Some cold, dingy cabin in the woods where he's been hiding out since he possessed Edmund. That man is one fruitcake, I tell you. Like bananapants wrapped in looney-toons."

I cuddled him closer, shuddering. "How the heck did he get his hands on you, Bel?"

"The way any deranged, hell-bent psychopath gets his hands on the familiar of the witch he thinks has done him wrong. He catches him by surprise. I came downstairs in the middle of the whole possession thing. Wow, is that ugly. There's lots of yelling and grunting and bones crunching. Yuck. Anyway, by the time I got a grip and realized what was happening, he'd snatched me up and took off. Then he locked me in some kinda crazy cage in that cabin and that was that. He put some kinda spell on me to keep my yap shut."

"A spell? So you missed all that?" I swung my finger in a circle, at the floor.

Bel chuckled. "I was sleepin' like a baby. Did you mop the floor with him, Boss?"

"*Dah*! She use all the skills we teach her. It was like watching Miikell Dumanovsky!"

"Who?" Win barked again.

"Forget it!" I interjected. "I don't care about anything but that Bel is here and safe."

"Ah, indeed. Dearest Belfry, I'm so relieved you're well, chap."

"Winterbutt! I'm so happy to hear you again, man!"

"Belfry, my bloke, it's good to have you home," Win said with warmth.

"Arkady Bagrov says double what Winterbutt says!"

"You mean ditto, my Siberian Terminator," Bel chirped on a giggle. "It's ditto, and ditto for me."

Whiskey barked his discontent, his howl now filled with desperation. "We're comin', little buddy!" Bel yelled.

I made a run for the stairs, following the barking until I found both Whiskey and Spike in one of the guest bedrooms. "Oh, Whiskey!"

He made a run at me, his bulky body thrusting against my knees, his tongue lolling from the side of his mouth. I knelt and wrapped my arms around his neck, squeezing him tight, still fighting off another batch of tears.

Bel flew from the safety of my shoulder and landed atop his friend's back. "There's my guy! Who's a good boy?" he sang.

Strike pecked his way toward us, waddling and clucking to brush against my arm, cooing in soft ripples of sound as I stroked his head.

"For the love of cats. We have a turkey, Boss? Seriously? A turkey? Where the heck did we get a turkey? It's like I can't even be kidnapped without your whole world falling apart or something."

"Yep. We have a turkey. Hey, did I ever tell you the story about how my familiar was kidnapped and my whole world blew up and all I got was this adorable turkey?"

We all laughed then—we laughed for a long time.

Together.

EPILOGUE

Christmas Day

"What a wonderful day, Dove. Full of family and friends. Good food, fantastic wine. Well done, Stephania."

I grinned and sighed. Yes. The food had been magnificent even without the turkeys I'd ordered.

Thank goodness for my parents, who could whip up a fresh turkey and all the trimmings with the blink of an eye. If not for them, I'd have had some serious explaining to do to Enzo and Carmella and I wouldn't have had the pleasure of learning how to roast a turkey to perfection.

Not to mention, they also knew how to ensure Edmund didn't remember a thing and was returned safely to his apartment, where his disappearance was explained away with car trouble in a remote area with no cell phone coverage. By the time my parents were done giving Edmund some false memories, he came off looking like a hero.

They were even more useful when it came to getting rid of that spell Kip had found on the Internet. The way it stood now, though, it looked like Ralph and Patty and their very high-priced, very savvy attorney might be able to get them off on the lesser charge of involuntary manslaughter.

I was grateful I didn't have to ask my parents to find a spell that would save them from a sentence of life in prison. It was, after all, my fault Adam Westfield made a deadly pastry designed to kill me, and I hated that my past had created something so horrible.

But as my father pointed out, they did leave the scene of a crime, and punishment was necessary.

"It all went as you planned, even with last night's little glitch, yes?"

"*Little glitch*? I'm not sure I'd call Adam Westfield possessing Edmund's body and kidnapping Bel a little glitch."

Win chuckled in my ear. "You handled yourself so well last night, I'd call him nothing more than a minor disruption, Mini-Spy."

I shivered as I remembered how terrified I'd been last night, but I shook it off and opted to revel in the warm glow of the remains of the day and the lights of our Christmas tree.

I hunkered down in my favorite chair by the fire-place with Belfry snuggled against my shoulder and Whiskey at my feet. Strike, who we'd somehow decided was now officially a part of the family, sat next to Whiskey, his wings tucked under his body as he slept.

I wasn't sure how we were going to handle a new addition of such an odd variety as Strike, but he was so sweet, I decided we'd figure it out—much the way we'd figured out our ghostly dynamic and each new surprise that had come along since Win and I met.

My sigh was content as Win and I sat together, sharing the last lingering moments of the best Christmas I'd ever had. My parents were well; sound asleep in guest bedrooms upstairs, healthy and happy. Bel was home where he belonged and I was never letting him out of my sight again; everyone I loved was safe and sound.

And Win was here.

"Did you look to see if Father Christmas left you something under the tree, Stephania?"

"Something for me?" I loved giving gifts, but I didn't need anything. I had everything I needed.

"You didn't think I'd let our first Christmas go by without commemorating it, did you?"

"Is it footie pajamas? You know how much I love a good footie with the flap in the back," I teased.

"I do, and I shudder at how awful your taste truly is. Footies, as you call them, are for farmers and toddlers. Go on now," he coaxed in his husky voice. "It's all the way in the back in the gold wrapping paper with the red bow.

I tucked Bel closer to my neck and slid from the chair, dropping to my knees to wiggle my way under the tree. My hand made contact with the smooth paper and the velvet bow almost instantly. I pulled it toward me with butterflies in my stomach.

Holding it up, a box no bigger than one might use to wrap underwear, I tried to make light of something that held so much meaning to me. I could never tell Win how special a gift from him was to my heart. I always thought of how awkward I would make him feel if I did. So I kept all my emotions tucked away. At least for now.

"Nice wrapping job, Spy Guy. Did you pay some-body to do this?"

"I most assuredly did—with Belfry's help, of course. I haven't achieved that particular skill as of yet. But it's certainly on my wish list of desired spirit skills."

I giggled, running my hands over the beautiful gold paper, treasuring the effort he'd put into giving me a gift.

"Well, get on with it, Dove," Win encouraged.

Slipping my finger under the edge, I tore the paper off until there was nothing but a box the color of black velvet. As I lifted the top, my breathing hitched and my throat tightened. "Oh, Win... It's beautiful... How did you..."

"Photoshop and Belfry. Our little bloke's quite gifted on the Internet."

I stared down at the beautiful sterling-silver picture frame with an embossed sign for infinity along the top and bottom and smiled at the picture.

A picture of us—me, Win, Bel and Whiskey.

"It's the sign for infinity," I whispered as I reached out and ran my thumb over the intertwining symbols.

"That's all of us, Dove. Never broken, never ending."

My heart tightened and constricted in my chest and my throat threatened to close up. "Yeah. That's us, Spy Guy."

Win's warmth surrounded me, tucking me close to his aura. "Merry Christmas, my dove."

"Merry Christmas, Win. The merriest yet."

Closing my eyes, I cherished this moment. One I knew in the deepest part of my heart would always be one of my most treasured.

The End
(I so hope you'll come back in the New Year and join Stevie, Win, Bel and the gang for an all new round of mysteries!)

PREVIEW ANOTHER BOOK BY DAKOTA CASSIDY

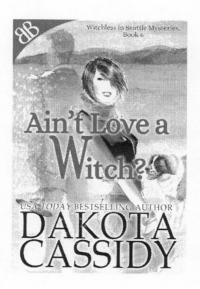

Chapter 1

"Oh, Dove, really? I'd rather face a firing squad deep in

the jungles of Gondwana than be forced to watch this," I complained to Stevie.

Yes, of course I know that sounds dire to you lot—a firing squad—maybe even melodramatic. But truly, gun to my head (and it was literally pointed at my head at the time), I would. Those hedonistic guerillas would be far easier to escape in my estimation, and certainly the colors and sounds coming from them wouldn't be quite as abrasive.

And as much as I love to indulge the most important woman in my life with her every whim, can you blame a man if he doesn't want to watch *My Big Fat American Gypsy Wedding?*

Stevie threw a piece of popcorn up in the air and charmingly caught it with her mouth before she said, "I can't help it. I can't look away. It's Saturday night and I've been Madam Zoltaring until my head spins with the tourist season in full swing. I need some mindless down time, and this provides. Plus, those dresses, right? They're almost unreal. Besides, don't you have women to chase on Plane Limbo to keep you entertained? No one's forcing you to watch my shame, you know."

I do not, in fact, have women to chase on Plane Limbo—the in between I'm stuck in until I can find a way to get back to the plane of the living. Actually, for accuracy's sake, there are plenty of female souls waiting to cross for various reasons, wandering the surface of the place I now call home. Some quite attractive souls, I might add.

However, they all pale in comparison to a soul who does not share the same space I do, and never will. Well, not for a terribly long time, I'd hope, or for as long as I can keep her safe, anyway. With her penchant for throwing herself into one murder investigation after another, keeping her safe has become dicey at best.

Anyway, since I died, I find chasing women is no longer what puts the lumps of sugar in my tea it once was. Bollocks. As a PS: I miss tea. Proper tea, mind you, not the sort they serve here in America. I certainly mean no offense by that statement, but tea differs greatly over the pond.

Suddenly, Stevie sat upright, her blue eyes squinting, and looked to the ceiling, where she frequently does when talking to me because she can't seem to break the habit, even though I think she knows I'm right next to her. As an FYI, I don't hover about the ceiling as one would think a ghost does. I sit next to her on the couch where it's comfortable, and where I can occasionally catch the delightful scent of her perfume or see the dent in the right side of her cheek when she smiles with impish delight.

"Wait, you faced a firing squad in Gondwana? Holy-schmoly, Secret Agent Man. That's a big ol' word. Plus, you lived to tell the tale?" She paused and gave a sheepish glance upward. "Well, at least you lived that one time, anyway."

Indeed, I had lived that one time. If only I'd lived the most important time. Alas, had I lived, I wouldn't be here right now, with this woman and my new band of friends.

I've decided there's a give and take, and sometimes, the take is bigger than the give.

Though, had I lived, I'd be off pursuing some other evil villain for MI6, instead of watching the telly and unheard by almost everyone around me save for Stevie. Of this you can be sure—I regret nothing.

"He did live, my little tiger lily of summer. Arkady see with his own eyes this man take on five thugs with guns to his head. He is quick like gazelle. Ah, you should have seen his dropkick somersault in air. Like matrix poetry!"

We all chuckled at Arkady's analogy. They are as bright and colorful as he.

Ah, my chap Arkady Bagrov—a good Russian bloke indeed. Of course, you all know we haven't always been friends, but in the afterlife, everything changes. Once lifelong enemies as agents from opposing countries, now Plane Limbo ghost brethren.

We both have the same goal in mind, protecting Stevie from harm, earthly or otherwise.

He's been quite a solid addition to our patched-together family of misfits. Two dead spies, a talking bat familiar, a handsome if not goofball St. Bernard named Whiskey, a turkey (yes, a turkey. He's actually a right sweet chap) named Strike we acquired during what shall forever be known as the Christmas From Hell of 2016 and, of course, Stevie, my near powerless witch. I use the adverb "near" because, despite the hateful act that took her powers, she's somehow managed to regain a very small, very limited amount of her witchness.

We'd found one another when each of our lives were in a state of rapid, very difficult transitions. I'd just died—or should I say, my ex-lover and former fellow spy had recently murdered me (more on that later). Stevie'd had her witch powers slapped out of her by a vengeful warlock and had recently returned to her hometown of Ebenezer Falls, WA, to lick her wounds with my man Belfry, her bat familiar, in tow.

Arkady came into our lives a good bit after, but he, too, had been alone, and now none of us were.

"You're my hero, Winterbutt. See me bat my eyelashes at you," Belfry quipped from Stevie's shoulder with a breathy sigh, his favorite place to rest.

I chuckled. "Stop, old chap, or you'll make me blush like a giddy schoolgirl who's been asked to dance for the first time at prom."

"I'd sure like to see that," Belfry chirped.

Ah. I'd like for him to see that, too. I'm sure I've mentioned I'm determined to reenter Stevie's plane. The longer I'm here in limbo, refusing to move past this plane and onto whatever lies beyond, and each time I see someone cross over into that magnificent light, the more determined I become.

I've done it successfully once—returned to Stevie's plane. It wasn't for long, mind you. It was only long enough to feel the soft press of Stevie's lips to mine, touch her silky skin, hold her in my arms, but it happened...and I'll never forget that moment.

Yet, if I didn't have enough incentive before that incredible moment, I do now. I managed to inhabit my twin brother's body while he was unconscious, and it drained the life out of me.

Hah! Little joke there. I have no life to drain, as you know. I suppose it's better to say the event drained my *energy*, but I managed it, and it brought me great hope moving forward. Since, I haven't been able to repeat my performance, but I won't give up. Not until I'm back on Stevie's plane where I belong. Also, as a note on the ethical care and treatment of a possession, be aware, I would never possess a body with deep earthly ties. For instance, I would never take over the body of a husband and father, or a body whose family and friends abound.

I know with clear certainty I couldn't wander about in the physical body of someone who would be deeply mourned, on the off chance we should ever run into a bereaved loved one. Nor would I ever take over a body where the soul, even weakly, still exists.

I have rules for this eventual possession, strict, unbending, ironclad rules, and when the right situation presents itself, the absolute right situation, I'll make my move.

I'll take that vow a step further in regard to my long-lost brother as well. We are identical, and I'm quite positive I could possess his earthly shell. But as angry as I am with his attempt to steal everything I left to Stevie, I refuse to possess his body while he still lives in a permanent play for life on this plane.

To note, I've not been able to locate my twin brother since he turned tail and ran after threatening to take everything I left to Stevie in my will. Likely, because for all the DNA he could produce, identical twins do not share the same fingerprints. When called upon to produce them in the presence of lawyers, my twin disappeared.

Still, the threat of having all my riches, all my worldly possessions in jeopardy after I'd bequeathed them to Stevie, was and remains, unacceptable. All this after she'd so graciously agreed to help me solve the murder of my lovely friend, Madam Zoltar—the only person on this plane who believed I wasn't some delusion in her mind.

We'd held our collective breath for quite some time, waiting to see if Balthazar would show back up, until we decided my twin had finally wised up and skulked back from whence he'd come. Yet, a great sadness comes with his disappearance for me personally, despite his dirty tactics. I would have liked to know Balthazar, hear his life story, possibly help heal the wounds caused by the time he'd spent in foster care during his youth, while I'd lived with and been nurtured by a loving family.

There's mystery surrounding our adoption and the reasons we were split up as infants. A mystery that went with my mother to her grave, which we can't find a hint of anywhere. Not even MI6 has any information about my true lineage. Though, come to find, they were thoroughly aware I'd been adopted. I was gobsmacked when I found out about my adoption, and remain as such to this day.

But there's no denying, Balthazar looks exactly like me, and yearns for what I have as though I somehow personally wronged him and stole the life he thinks he should have been given.

Yet, I have no grudge to bear with Balthazar. I'm saddened by his callous disregard for me. Surely twins have a connection no other form of sibling share, no? I've read much on the subject of twindom, and while I can't ever remember feeling as though anything were missing from my life, that certainly doesn't mean had I known of his existence, I would have attempted to rob him blind the way he did me and, by proxy, Stevie.

Ahem. Maybe my backside's a little more chapped than I'd care to admit.

Regardless, he's not in the picture right now, and while it pains me to consider he's what you Americans call a loose cannon, I can't fret over what I can't see.

"Win?" Stevie called my name on a yawn.

"Yes, Dove."

"Did you remember to put out the word up there for Mr. Piscatello?"

"The chap looking for his pig, Cris P. Bacon?" That's really what the bloke named his pig, ladies and gentleman. Stevie takes every single client seriously, no matter what they're looking for.

Arkady, Bel, and I? Not so much. I think we secretly

laughed for over an hour about this man and his pig. Call us heathens, but he's looking for his pig.

I repeat. *His pig.*

The guilt I feel over the three of us cackling like hyenas on a bender is enormous, if that makes our laughing any less horrible. Of course, I realize one can become attached to the oddest things. Take our turkey Strike, for instance. We adore him. But we had a good hen fest of a laugh about him, too.

Stevie stabbed her finger in the air as she tucked her feet under her. "That's him. And before you say it, I know. Believe me, I know. It's a pig. He wants to contact his pig. Ridiculous, right? But what if it were Whiskey or Strike? Wouldn't you want to know they made it over the Rainbow Bridge? Chris P. was just as important to him as our pets are to us. No matter what species."

I gave Arkady the sternest spy look I possessed when he hissed the beginnings of his hearty chuckle. "Of course, Dove. I love them as much as you do. However, I don't know if there *is* a Rainbow Bridge. I've never seen this bridge animal lovers speak of. I've never met anything other than humans here on Plane Limbo, and neither Arkady nor I have been able to locate Mr. Bacon—which is of course unfortunate, but the truth."

Stevie sat back on the couch, deflated. "I might have to cancel with him then. Bel, would you put that in the calendar for me, please? Shoot. I really hoped we'd be able to help. I'm not sure what I'll do if there's really no

Rainbow Bridge. Surely the man upstairs doesn't abandon the furbabies? I refuse to believe that. It's unconscionable."

That's my girl. Heart of an angel, mind like a steel trap.

"I promise Arkady and I will hunt high and low for the Rainbow Bridge if it eases your mind, Dove. Won't we, old chap?"

"Dah! Whatever you wish, my fluffy Twinkie of love. I live to serve you and only you, *malutka*."

Stevie smiled up into the ceiling the way she always did when Arkady used a food endearment to reassure her. The smile she didn't realize was reserved for only those closest and dearest to her. It held extra warmth in its creases and made her brilliant eyes glow.

"Thank you, Arkady. I can't bear the idea animals don't cross over, too. It's unfair." Lifting her arms, she stretched and yawned before turning off the telly. "I think it's time I hit the hay. I can't believe I'm saying this, but I'll be glad when tourist season is over. Swear, I'm tired of people asking me if I can tell them what the lottery numbers will be for next week. Does no one take a medium seriously anymore? We talk to dead people—we don't see the future!"

"It has been a busy season for you, Stephania. But look at all the money donated to the animal shelter and the hospital. You've made quite an impact."

That made her smile. This smile was different, though. It was the smile of pride, one that said she was happy we could contribute by donating all her reading fees to various charities, and she'd work as hard as she had to in order to keep the donations flowing. Stevie refused to rest on her laurels—something she surely could have done after inheriting all of my money.

Yet, Stephania has an incredible work ethic, one she made very clear to me from the start when I suggested she buy a real Gucci gown and not some used, vintage thrift store aberration. She refused my free ride and continues to do so.

And that's just one of the things I lo— *Cherish* about her, and her overly large heart.

As she gathered herself, Bel, and Whiskey to head to bed, her adorable bear slippers flopping a path to the stairs, I felt that undeniable wall go up between us. The one we'd erected out of respect for her privacy.

Yes, yes. I can peek in on her anytime I choose. When she's sleeping, when she's putting on her makeup, whenever. But I don't. I absolutely adhere to a strict code of honor where Stevie's concerned. I would never risk her discontent for my own advantage. Her privacy is important to me. Thus, I behave as though I've just dropped her at her front door after a lovely outing unless it's an emergency.

Still, I feel this invisible wall far more than I suspected I would. It's the wall separating our worlds.

Maybe it's only my melancholy, but it's there. It's always there.

As she began to creep up the stairs, Whiskey in tow, she whispered, "Night, Win. Night, Arkady. Sweet dreams…"

"Good night, John-Boy. Good night, Mary-Helen—"

"That's Mary Ellen, old man."

Stevie's laughter tinkled in my ears as she hit the top of the steps and made a right toward her bedroom.

I sighed as Arkady slapped me on the back.

Oh, something else to note. Yes, Arkady and I can indeed *see* one another as though we were still alive. We can feel one another's touch—in fact, we even occasionally keep our spy skills honed with some hand-to-hand combat.

All in jest, of course, but some of the inhabitants of Plane Limbo don't fancy our tussling about the lush hills and valleys as they determine whether they should cross. This is a place of reverence; a place to reflect and make the most important decision one will ever make. The lovely Mrs. Pederson reprimanded us once after a particularly vocal joust.

It should also be noted, Arkady has no desire to return to Stevie's plane. He claims to be done with all earthly matters. To a degree, I understand. A spy's life is treacherously hard and involves things like deception and all manner of bomb paraphernalia, and lest we forget, little time for anything but spying. Spies don't have families, or house and car payments unless it's an undercover assignment.

Thus, Arkady's chosen to rest now, and I support that choice entirely.

We also don't sleep, which I find terribly disappointing. I missed my fair share of naps as an adult due to my line of work; you'd think the unfairness of that would be given a balance here on Plane Limbo.

Anyway, it leaves us with much time on our hands.

"You okey-doke, my friend?" he asked as we sat together where we always sit. On a bench in a park with cherry blossom trees that eternally bloom and the greenest grass I've ever seen.

His sharply defined face with thick dark brows, offset by a longish nose, cheery green eyes and, if you can believe it, a handlebar moustache and goatee, were once the perfect cover for his deadly skills, and when he looked at me the way he was right now, I avoided making eye contact.

Arkady was always a hit with all the ladies, with his deep chestnut hair in a topknot and his melodic accent. His muscular body, in the shape of a T, drove them all wild. I often compared his almost perfectly proportioned body to a newer millennial version of the weightlifters once so prevalent in the circus; only rather than tights he wore his tight T-shirts and jeans.

Yet, he had a way with people. He made you feel like he was someone you might sit and share a pint with, thinking he'd listen to your woes. But make no mistake, in life, he was revered as a spy.

But nowadays, here on Plane Limbo, he was simply Arkady. I chuckled, slapping him about the shoulders. "I'm okey-doke, chap. What shall we do tonight while our mini-spy rests her lovely head? Chess, perhaps? No. We just played last night. Let's mix it up a bit, shall we? How about backgammon? Shuffleboard?"

"Why do we not speak of how you are feeling, Zero?"

Zero, if you're wondering, was my spy code name. Zero Below—because I was considered cold as ice.

If only MI6 could see me now. I'm tepid at best, if we're to rate me by their standards.

"What shall we speak about, Arkady?"

He wrinkled his round nose up and made a face, squeezing my chin with his beefy hand. "Bah! You do this to avoid. Do not play mousecat with me. I know how you are really feeling. You must say it so we can talk about it, friend."

"It's cat and mouse, mate. And I'm not playing at anything, good sir. I don't know what the bloody—"

The doorbell rang just then, sending us both to our feet, for all the good it would do, but you can't teach an old spy new tricks.

"Who is this who rings doorbell so late at the night? Has no one make with the manners here in America?"

Stevie's head poked around the corner of the hall upstairs. "Seriously? Is that the doorbell at this time of night?"

"'Twas indeed, Mini-Spy. Shall we investigate as I've taught you?"

As she came into full view, her shoulders slumped beneath her bunnies-hopping-over-rainbows bathrobe —my favorite garment of hers, by the way—she whined, "Aw, c'mon, Spy Guy. Don't make me put on the helmet. I've only been hit on the head once. I'm much better at this now. Plus, we have a security system."

"Stephania, I won't have your skull bashed in due to your pride! Get the helmet and get it now!" I didn't realize I was shouting until I had, and if I didn't notice after that, there was always Stevie with her eyes of fire to remind me.

She skipped down the steps and wagged a finger at the ceiling even though I was right beside her. "Don't you tell me what to do, Winterbutt. I'm not wearing that helmet or the kneepads or that ridiculous mouth guard you ordered. You're being way too overprotective. When was the last mission you took that involved a mouth guard?"

All right, she had me there. However, she'd never had to witness me almost dying, unable to do a single thing about it but wait helplessly as I crumple to the ground while some madman fiendishly hovers over me. I *have* watched as she'd almost died, and I have no wish to do so again. Thus, I encourage safety.

"Exactly my point, hall monitor," she said to the ceiling, crossing her arms over her chest in defensive Stephania mode. "Now can it, pal, and let me look at the security camera."

"Dah, even you must admit the mouth guard is too much, Zero. It is as my little summer squash says, it makes her lips feel flappy when she take it out. You do not want her lips to be *more* flappy, do you, eh?"

I narrowed my eyes at my good mate and signaled him to put a sock in it, but he just grinned that wide grin of his that takes up his whole face, and once was accompanied by a bullet to your brain.

"You can it, too, Russian, or I'll make you watch *Mission Impossible* again with my flappy lips commentating the whole way. Hear me?"

Arkady groaned long and low, letting his head hang to his barrel-like chest. "Ack! Please do not make me suffer that Tom Boat person and his pretty-girl face that never even sees a single tooth missing on his *spy missions*," he spat.

Arkady has little regard for American spy films and shares his opinion quite frequently, calling the stars Candy Boys.

"That's Tom Cruise, buddy, and I'll make you watch them all back to back if you don't behave!" Stevie warned.

Now I grinned at Arkady, devilishly, of course.

On tiptoe, Stevie peered out the front door's stained glass and shook her head before looking at the footage of the live feed on the laptop in the dining room. She cocked her mussed head and said, "Huh. Nothing."

I let out a sigh of relief. Thank heavens there'd be no attempted assassinations on her life today.

And then we all stopped and tilted our ears in the direction of the door in order to listen.

"Win?"

I listened once more before I said, "Hmmm?"

"Do you hear what I hear?"

"What did you hear, Dove?"

She bit the inside of her cheek. She does that when she's thinking, and it's quite adorable. "I could swear—"

And there it was again, a soft mewling, one that grew and turned into a swell of sound sure to rival the scream of the whistle atop the Orient Express.

Before anyone could protest—before I could once more warn Stephania not to behave with such foolish impulse, she flung the door open.

And right there, directly on the welcome mat that read "Wipe Your Paws," was a baby carrier. One you'd put in a car, I believe.

And inside this blue and white baby carrier was a dark-haired cherub with blushed cheeks and pudgy fists I often hear women coo they'd like to nibble.

And attached to that baby's pastel-blue blanket with the satin hem was a note that read—

My darling Winsical (remember our little joke, Win?),
Meet your beautiful baby boy!

NOTE FROM DAKOTA

I do hope you enjoyed this book, I'd so appreciate it if you'd help others enjoy it, too.

Recommend it. Please help other readers find this book by recommending it.

Review it. Please tell other readers why you liked this book by reviewing it at online retailers or your blog. Reader reviews help my books continue to be valued by distributors/resellers. I adore each and every reader who takes the time to write one!

If you love the book or leave a review, please email **dakota@dakotacassidy.com** so I can thank you with a personal email. Your support means more than you'll ever know! Thank you!

ABOUT THE AUTHOR

Dakota Cassidy is a USA Today bestselling author with over thirty books. She writes laugh-out-loud cozy mysteries, romantic comedy, grab-some-ice erotic romance, hot and sexy alpha males, paranormal shifters, contemporary kick-ass women, and more.

Dakota was invited by Bravo TV to be the Bravo-holic for a week, wherein she snarked the hell out of all the Bravo shows. She received a starred review from Publishers Weekly for Talk Dirty to Me, won a Romantic Times Reviewers' Choice Award for Kiss and Hell, along with many review site recommended reads and reviewer top pick awards.

Dakota lives in the gorgeous state of Oregon with her real-life hero and her dogs, and she loves hearing from readers!

OTHER BOOKS BY DAKOTA CASSIDY

Visit Dakota's website at
http://www.dakotacassidy.com for more information.

A Lemon Layne Mystery, a Contemporary Cozy Mystery Series

    1. Prawn of the Dead

    2. Play That Funky Music White Koi

    3. Total Eclipse of the Carp

Witchless In Seattle Mysteries, a Paranormal Cozy Mystery series

    1. Witch Slapped

    2. Quit Your Witchin'

    3. Dewitched

    4. The Old Witcheroo

    5. How the Witch Stole Christmas

    6. Ain't Love a Witch

    7. Good Witch Hunting

Nun of Your Business Mysteries, a Paranormal Cozy Mystery series

1. Then There Were Nun
2. Hit and Nun

Wolf Mates, a Paranormal Romantic Comedy series

1. An American Werewolf In Hoboken
2. What's New, Pussycat?
3. Gotta Have Faith
4. Moves Like Jagger
5. Bad Case of Loving You

A Paris, Texas Romance, a Paranormal Romantic Comedy series

1. Witched At Birth
2. What Not to Were
3. Witch Is the New Black
4. White Witchmas

Non-Series

Whose Bride Is She Anyway?
Polanski Brothers: Home of Eternal Rest
Sexy Lips 66

Accidentally Paranormal, a Paranormal Romantic Comedy series

Interview With an Accidental—a free introductory guide to the girls of the Accidentals!

1. The Accidental Werewolf
2. Accidentally Dead
3. The Accidental Human
4. Accidentally Demonic
5. Accidentally Catty
6. Accidentally Dead, Again

7. The Accidental Genie

8. The Accidental Werewolf 2: Something About Harry

9. The Accidental Dragon

10. Accidentally Aphrodite

11. Accidentally Ever After

12. Bearly Accidental

13. How Nina Got Her Fang Back

14. The Accidental Familiar

15. Then Came Wanda

16. The Accidental Mermaid

The Hell, a Paranormal Romantic Comedy series

1. Kiss and Hell

2. My Way to Hell

The Plum Orchard, a Contemporary Romantic Comedy series

1. Talk This Way

2. Talk Dirty to Me

3. Something to Talk About

4. Talking After Midnight

The Ex-Trophy Wives, a Contemporary Romantic Comedy series

1. You Dropped a Blonde On Me

2. Burning Down the Spouse

3. Waltz This Way

Fangs of Anarchy, a Paranormal Urban Fantasy series

1. Forbidden Alpha

2. Outlaw Alpha

Made in the USA
Monee, IL
04 May 2020

26543830R00143